Squirrels

The

Mutation

A Novel By

Hank Patterson

The characters, places, events, and situations in this book are purely fictional. Any resemblance to actual persons, living or dead, is coincidental and not intended by the author.

ISBN: 1-4140-3211-0 (e-book)
ISBN: 1-4140-3210-2 (Paperback)
ISBN: 1-4140-3209-9 (Dust Jacket)

This book is printed on acid free paper.

1stBooks - rev. 01/29/04

This book is dedicated in loving memory to my grandmother Thelma Warfield, grandfather Clarence Warfield and my father Henry Patterson. May you all continue to soar with the angels!

Acknowledgements

First, I would like to thank my Lord and Savior Jesus Christ for all of the blessings he has bestowed upon me. I would like to send a deep thanks to my family, Ronda, Terrez and Jasmine. My wife, son and daughter provided the continuous support, patience and encouragement that helped to see me though this challenging project. Kudos goes out to Big George for his artistic views. A special shout out goes to the crew Porter, Tash and Shannon who inspired me to write this book. To my mom Joan Patterson, as a mother does and you always do thanks for that push and surge of energy you gave when I thought all was lost. A loving thanks to you, you are my rock. George and Candy thanks for being there. Debra (sis) love you! I would also like to thank my typist Debra who put the written work into a legible form. A very special thanks to my editor Cathy Stephens for helping me put it all together. God Bless you all. To my reader's thanks and look for more books soon.

Chapter 1

Today was like any other Saturday morning in Newton, Iowa. Terrez, one of the locals, an eight-year old, was pondering what he should do today. His mother an accountant with the Barns and Slaughter Mortgage Company was up early fixing breakfast. His father Hank was out at the local track running his normal two miles like every Saturday morning. Jasmine, his thirteen-year-old sister had a sleepover last night so the house was full this morning. Her cousins Porter, eleven; Antasha, twelve, who was Porter's best friend and their other cousin, nine year old Shannon. They spent most of the night watching horror movies. The girls along with Hank liked gross movies blood and guts; even Terrez was starting to like them. Three weeks ago, Terrez and his father were riding through different neighborhoods looking at homes; Hank would do that periodically to get ideas for his own landscaping. What they saw this morning would stick in their minds forever.

The Newton General Hospital was busy this Saturday morning, Ronda, Hank's wife had just finished cooking breakfast and called the kids to the table when the phone rang, it was Miko. Miko was Ronda's younger sister; she worked as a Nurse's Assistant at the hospital. She was calling to see how her daughter Shannon was doing. Ronda told her she was doing fine and that the kids were having breakfast. Miko had worked late last night and was still in bed but she had to tell someone what she discovered at work. While making her rounds on the fifth floor, checking the charts for the nurses, she heard strange noises coming from the floor above. This was not the first time she had heard these noises. When she asked some of the nurses on that floor about the sounds they told her that it was the wind or something because that floor had been closed for years.

The story was that one of the doctors had been caught trying to clone animals in the back room of one of the labs. Miko got the keys to one of the locked doors from one of her friends Mike, who worked for a janitorial company that was contracted to clean the hospital. He made her promise not to tell anyone he had given her keys to that floor since he had stole them about six months ago. His boss Lou, a fat middle-aged man with a red beard and short red hair was at lunch. He left the keys in the janitor's office in the basement. Miko took the key to Lab 621.

Hank came in from his morning run and motioned to Ronda that he wanted to talk to her about something he saw on the way to the track. Terrez finished his breakfast and asked his father if he could go outside. He took his B-B gun, a Christmas gift his father bought him a couple of years ago against his mother's warning. Hank's mother JP, which was short for Joann Peterson, was a very attractive woman. She was in her early sixties, looked about forty with light clear skin and rounded very well. She had retired three years ago as a top executive of one of the major car companies and was pretty well off. She lived alone, her husband died a very long time ago and she never remarried. JP had a nice home with a pool and a pet dog, a Sharpei. Red-dog is what the family named him. He was an excellent watchdog and was very good with the kids when they visited. JP would always remind Hank of his first and last B-B gun, which she was sorry she had ever bought. When Hank was ten years old, he and some of his friends were out walking in the alley, shooting squirrels off the wires and fences. One of the neighborhood boys Tony suggested they play war games. "How are we going to protect ourselves from being shot?" Hank had asked simply. Tony replied, "We'll use garbage can tops to protect us." While playing Pete got shot in the eye, it was a bloody mess Hank could still remember the screams, the blood pouring down Pete's face through his fingers and the whipping they got. Pete ended up with a glass eye. He and his family moved to another state shortly after the accident.

Terrez asked again if he could go outside; his father told him yes and reminded him not to point the gun at anyone. Ronda was off the phone now and wanted to talk about what Miko had shared with her during the conversation. The girls were finished eating and Ronda told them to go outside too. It was a beautiful Saturday and the forecast was mid 70's with clear skies. Jasmine suggested they go to the park and all the girls agreed except Tash. She saw Terrez go outside with his gun and wanted to go with him. Terrez didn't mind so he waited in the back until she came out.

"Ronda," Hank said to his wife, "I can't believe how many dead squirrels were on the road this morning, a lot more than normal." It brought back memories of the morning he and Terrez were riding through Sherfield, a wooded area with huge homes where mostly doctors and lawyers lived. That's when they saw it. In front of one of the homes on a street called Somerset they saw a giant squirrel about ten or twelve feet tall, carved out of one of the trees. It looked so real that it gave him the chills. Just as they were leaving the area, it started storming. When they were almost off of Somerset, a strange assortment of lighting bolts appeared out of nowhere. It looked as if they hit the squirrel but the squirrel stood tall. This was impossible he thought to himself. By now Terrez was horrified, he had always been scared of thunder and lightening. His father pulled him closer and told him that they would be home in a few minutes. Those few minutes seemed like an eternity to Terrez who was now shaking because the storm was getting worse. "What an idiot I must be dragging my son out in this mess," Hank, said. How was he to know this would be one of the worst storms to hit the area in years? The news said possible T-Storms later that evening, but as usual they were wrong. Hank often wondered how they could be wrong most of the time and never lose their jobs. He pulled up in the driveway and could see Terrez had calmed down a little. That day, the rain, thunder and lighting never let up. The storm knocked out most of Newton's residential electric service but the Petersons would be spared this day.

Chapter 2

Miko told her sister of the strange sounds coming from the sixth floor and how she got the keys from a co-worker whom she did not name. "Last night she told me she snuck up to the sixth floor," Ronda explained to her husband. When Miko got to the sixth floor, it was very dark and quiet. She wondered what she was doing there all alone. She began to feel uneasy as if something bad was going to happen. Mike told her the lights up there didn't work so she took a flashlight with her. The hallway was empty and there were a lot of doors. She tried one, Lab 612 and it was locked. She fumbled with the keys until she found the right one, just then the gnawing began, it was very faint—not coming from the room she was in. I'll check it out next, Miko thought, but for now I want to know what's in this lab and why had this floor really been closed down? The lab appeared empty except for some large racks toward the back that had very large bottles on them. She walked slowly toward the back and the gnawing started again. This time it was louder, Miko stood completely still, she was beginning to shake a little it stopped. Miko could see there was something inside the bottles that were actually jars, Hank," Ronda explained, seeming really nervous. "She told me that they had"—and at that very moment Jasmine and Shannon burst in the door screaming and crying. "My God what happened, Oh, my God," Ronda shrieked.

Terrez and Tash had been walking through the alley when one of the neighborhood boys TJ, called out to them, "Hey, where you going?" he asked. "Down to the ravines," they called back. TJ was a little white kid who played with Terrez now and then. His parents worked for one of the car plants in town. He was nine years old and loved his video games, "Wait up, I'll come with you." The three of them made their way down into the ravines; you could hear the insects and the birds chirping; at that moment Terrez said, "Sshh, look up there," he pointed. There were two squirrels chasing each other in the trees. Terrez cocked his gun and aimed, POW!—The gun went crack; they heard the B-B strike the tree, he missed. "Let me see," Tash said. "No wait a minute." The squirrels were very still now looking towards the children, he took aim again, Tash and TJ looked on being very still, very quiet. POW! The gun went, thud it sounded, blood squirted from one of the squirrels. Terrez had hit it right between the eyes, the squirrel fell from the tree, the other stood very still then took off very quickly jumping from branch to branch, tree to tree. "Yes!" the kids exclaimed. "Did you see that? I hit him right between the eyes." "Yeah," said TJ and Tash. "I'm next," TJ said. "No you're not, I am," Tash replied. They began walking further into the woods looking for their prey…squirrels.

Chapter 3

Back on 2411 Somerset Street, a young doctor named Lou Spellman, lived alone, had very few friends and almost no visitors. He was reading over some papers in his home that he had recently transferred from Bedford Hospital, which was about ninety miles from Newton General. His neighbors thought he was strange because he didn't speak to anyone and kept late hours. You could see lights blinking in the basement almost every night, not to mention what was an eyesore out in front of the house. The house had been empty for the last ten years, before then, another doctor; an elderly man by the name of Josh Jackson lived there with his second wife, a young women in her thirties. His first wife had become very ill and died from unknown causes. Josh insisted on caring for her himself. Doctor Jackson also worked at Newton.

Meanwhile, at Hank and Ronda Peterson's house they were trying to calm the girls. "What happened at the park?" their mother asked. Shannon was still sobbing and appeared to be very frightened and upset so Ronda gave her some milk and cookies. She threw them up all over the kitchen table. "We better give Miko a call," Hank said. Ronda took Shannon upstairs to one of the four bedrooms and she went to sleep immediately. Hank called Miko she was coming over to get her daughter. Jasmine sat on the family sofa and waited to tell her story. Both her mother and father had returned now and she began… "We rode our bikes up to the park." The park set off in the middle of the suburban community of Newton in a community called Crow Hills. Like any other day at the park children played on the swings and slides. There was a baseball game going on, Porter went to watch the game and didn't see what happened. She was the last to get to the house and was waiting to hear about what was going on. Jasmine explained, that she and Shannon were playing catch with a football when a lot of crows started circling the area making loud noises. “They flew in and out of the trees but you couldn’t see what they were doing,” she said. “Then I threw the ball and it hit one of the branches and something fell out of the tree. We went to see what it was and when we got close it was a bloody hand that had been picked to the bones. We got scared and started running and screaming.” Porter saw them running and followed. Hank decided they better call the sheriff.

Chapter 4

Ever since that terrible rainstorm three weeks ago Hank had a funny feeling things were starting to change in Newton but he couldn't quite put his finger on it. The Sheriff arrived shortly after. The trio returned to the park where the girls spotted the hand. His name was Tyrone Brown, a short black stocky man who had the appearance of a weight lifter. He was married to a white woman and they had one child by the name of Casey who attended Jasmine's school. Hank met and talked with the Sheriff at one of the PTA meetings earlier that year.

Casey had been at the park that day too and told his father about the crows. He had been playing baseball on the other side. Jasmine led the two men to the spot where the hand was. There was barely anything left of it. Not far away Hank spotted something a bit strange. Two crows were chasing and pecking at a squirrel. "Mr. Peterson," the Sheriff called out, "I'm going to have my people take these remains to the lab so we can try to put this thing together. It appears the crows may have found this hand and bought it here." "Who do you think this could have possibly belonged to?" Hank asked. "Don't know, we'll check for any missing persons and try to get some prints but from the looks of this I don't see how that's going to be possible. In the meantime, it's getting late so you might want to take your daughter back home." At that moment Hank realized Terrez hadn't come home yet. He grabbed Jasmine, pulled out his cell phone and headed for the car.

Chapter 5

Terrez, Tash and TJ had turned back now and were heading home. It was just about dusk when they spotted another squirrel. TJ grabbed the B-B gun from Terrez and started shooting. "Stop," shouted Tash, "Let's go!" The squirrel ran off into the residential area where they were coming out of the woody ravines. The kids chased the squirrel down a block where there were no trees or fences. The squirrel being trapped ran up a street sign and had nowhere else to go. The three closed in, at that moment the squirrel let out a shriek and jumped off the pole right towards TJ. TJ dropped the gun, threw his hands over his head and turned away. The next thing Terrez saw was the squirrel biting TJ on the back of the neck. TJ was screaming and blood was squirting everywhere. Tash started running, Terrez was right behind her. “Help me,” TJ screamed as he tried to get the squirrel off his neck. He fell to the ground. Just then, Hank pulled around the corner, saw the boy on the ground and hopped out of the car. He darted toward TJ, grabbed the squirrel off him and slammed it to the ground stomping it to death. He picked the boy off the ground carrying him in both arms and put him in the back seat. TJ was in shock and not moving. “Call your mother,” he screamed to Jasmine and whipped the car around. “Tell her to call TJ’s mother and have her meet us at the hospital.” Terrez and Tash ran up to the front door of the house.

Chapter 6

It was getting late now and JP had just come in from a friend's retirement party. She had forgot to bring Red-Dog in before she'd left out earlier, a few more minutes was not going to hurt. It was time to get out of the dress and shoes her feet were starting to ache. Just as she slipped on her sweat pants, she heard a loud crash against the sliding door that led into the back yard. It frightened her and she stood still, suddenly Red-Dog began to bark wildly as if he had something. There was the sound of another animal; they were running around the back yard knocking over plants, chairs and making an awful noise. It came again—BAM! Against the window, now she wasn't sure what was out there. Her first thought was to open the door and take a look but she quickly decided not to try that, Red-Dog might have a burglar. "Call Hank" was her next thought. She dialed his number—no answer. She tried again often; she called, the kids would be on the other line and not click over. "Please God, someone answer." At that moment the noise stopped but she was still very frightened. She hadn't wanted to call the Sheriff because the neighbors often complained about Red-Dog's excessive barking and once she was fined one hundred dollars. Then it started again, she lay very still and was very frightened, "What had Red-Dog gotten a hold to, or what had gotten him?"

Mike got a call from Lou to come to work early. He wondered why since the company hardly ever gave up overtime. Lou also got a call from Dr. Going, the hospital's Chief of Operations. Some of the patients were starting to believe they heard noises from the floor above. "Come in and have a seat, would you like a cup of coffee or perhaps some tea?" "No thanks," Lou responded. Lou always had a couple of drinks at lunch and he would sneak sips during working hours. This was not the first time he had been called into the office. "Lou, I thought you were going to get some traps and poison for those fucking mice or rats or whatever is up there on six making that godforsaken gnawing noise. I'm trying to run a fucking hospital and I can't have nasty little rodents running around the goddamn place. This is supposed to be a clean environment." "Yes sir," Lou said, "we did lay some traps." "Well, get some stronger ones, I want that noise stopped." At that moment the phone rang and Dr. Going waved his hand at Lou to leave. He knew Lou had a drinking problem and wanted him out of the building but Klean & Klean was his sister's company and Lou was married to her.

Mike had arrived and was heading down to the office in the basement; Lou was waiting for him. "What's up?" Mike said as he took a seat. "Mike, I need some help, Going's on my ass about that noise up on six, it's started up again." "Yeah, I heard, what is it?" "Don't know. Sounds like some rats or something. You did lay those traps didn't you?" "Yeah, I told you I did when you asked me that two weeks ago, remember?" "What about Lab 621?" "What about it," Mike said, "I told you I couldn't get in and you have the keys. Open the door." "When I tried last time your key didn't work." Lou tried the keys himself last week and knew he'd lost them. The problem was he gets so drunk he can't remember anything and Mike knew this too.

"By the way am I getting paid for being here? I don't work or come in early for free." He got up and left. "Damn it," Lou struck his hand on the desk. "What did I do with that fucking key," he moaned to himself.

Chapter 7

In the early 1970's Josh Jackson was an astounding young doctor at Wayne State Medical Center in Detroit, Michigan with a great future ahead of him. He won numerous awards and world recognition for his research in cloning and regeneration. It was at one of those award presentations that Josh met his first wife. Her name was Lisa Straub she was a beautiful young blonde with slender legs that gave her the appearance of being tall. She had a thin nose and thin pink lips that seemed to glow whenever she spoke. Lisa was a Science Professor at Wayne State Science Center; she too admired Josh's discoveries. Josh had also heard of Lisa's work. She taught and did research in several fields that appealed to him. There had been an article on her in one of the local papers about her work in congenial disorders. She believed that using certain DNA from the fetus could prevent congenial disorders worldwide. The problem was that laws in the States prohibited her from doing certain testing. Josh was having the same problem; U.S. laws prohibited human cloning. Lisa and Josh believed that by mixing some animal DNA with human DNA they could cure some of the world's deadliest diseases.

Josh had been watching her from across the room. She had on a stunning black dress that spouted her nipples to full attention. He wore a black tuxedo. Later that evening the two met at the punch bowl. "Hello," Josh was the first to speak—"wonderful night." "Hi and congratulations on the award. I've been admiring your research for quite some time, I'm Lisa…" "Professor Lisa Straub, I know. I have a confession Lisa, I've been meaning to contact you for some time about some of your theories but with all these appearances I simply haven't had the time." "No time like the present, Dr. Jackson," Lisa added. "Josh, please call me Josh, Professor Straub." "Only if you call me, Lisa." "It's a deal, now, can we get out of here? These gatherings bore me to death."

"Likewise Doctor, I'm sorry—Josh. Where would you like to go?" "I was hoping we could go to my place." "Now you wouldn't be trying to make a pass at a girl would you?" "Of course." "Good, then let's go."

Josh lived in a plush house in Grosse Pointe. He made good money off of those boring appearances and from numerous speaking affairs around the country. "Nice," she thought to herself, "here was this renowned doctor interested in my work and not bad looking either." Josh was a bulking man about 6'2, black hair, slightly green eyes that seem to change colors. Both were single at the time and neither was involved with anyone. "Would you care for a drink?" Josh asked. "Yes, wine if you have some." "Of course, make yourself at home; I'll just be a minute." When he returned, Lisa was sitting on the love seat, legs crossed and gleaming. "Here you are my dear." "Thank you," Lisa nodded. Josh sat his wine down and walked around the couch. The next thing Lisa felt was his strong hand massaging the back of her neck. "That feels great." "Well come with me then." He grabbed her hand and the bottle of wine. "Grab those glasses dear." "Josh I don't know." "Don't be silly it'll be great, just what the doctor ordered." Lisa, was really nervous now she wasn't ready to just hop in bed with Josh although, she was attracted to him. Josh cut the light on and in the corner Lisa could see a huge Jacuzzi. On the other side of the room was this huge bed. Josh hit the switch on the wall, the Jacuzzi started bubbling and steam rose from within. "You can change in there." Josh pointed to a bathroom next to the Jacuzzi. "I don't have a swimming suit." "It's okay I won't bite." Lisa really wanted to get in so she went into the bathroom and quickly returned wrapped fully in a towel. Josh was already in the Jacuzzi sipping his wine. He had turned on some light music. Lisa walked up the stairs and down into the water. She knew Josh was looking so she slowly removed her towel revealing her thighs and breast for only a brief moment. "Have some more wine?" "Yes please." They were both feeling a pleasant uneasy kind of tension. Josh looked into Lisa's eyes sat down his glass and disappeared under the bubbling water. Lisa felt his head between her thighs and his lips on her vagina. She relaxed and opened her legs a little wider. Josh kissed her in a way there that she had never been kissed before. She licked her lips and her temperature was quickly rising. She forgot that he was still underwater until he suddenly emerged from below. "Josh," it was to late he'd gone down again and her whole body trembled from within. She wanted him inside her. She wanted to feel this big strong man hold and take control of the burning desire he had awakened. Josh rose again this time he stood all the way up and she could see from his knees up. He was so hard, so big she wanted him now. Josh grabbed her pulled her to him and gave her a gentle soft passionate wet kiss. He stepped out of the jacuzzi and she followed. Josh picked Lisa up in his strong secure arms. His penis stood straight and at attention. He carried her to his bed laid her down and climbed into the bed with her. Josh rolled on top of her covering her body with kisses and caresses. He slid inside her wet pulsating vagina, where with each thrust they both lost sight of time and space. Lisa knew that in the morning she would have to tell him, that she would be leaving the country for an undisclosed period of time. But, tonight she intended to enjoy every inch of him.

Josh got up early and had already fixed breakfast. Lisa strolled into the kitchen following the smells of coffee, bacon and eggs. "Good morning gorgeous, did you sleep well?" "Good morning, yes like a log. Josh last week I received a research grant to study the effects of hybridization of squirrels in Southern Asia." Asia was known for its giant and tricolor tree squirrels and their nocturnal flying squirrels. "That's wonderful," Josh exclaimed. "What I wouldn't do to get over there; the damn laws here in the States have me at a standstill." "Well, I'm putting a small team together. I'd love to have you but what about your work here? How could you just pick up and leave?" "Actually, I was planning to leave Michigan anyway, there's nothing left for me to do at the school, money's not an issue so I've just been looking for the right project." "Then, it's settled we leave in three months."

Chapter 8

Lou Spellman was working a double that Saturday when TJ had been bitten by the squirrel. Hank called the sheriff in route to the hospital and told him what had happen. “A squirrel! A squirrel? You’ve got to be fucking kidding me.” “Tell that to this little kid in my back seat. Call the hospital, tell them what happened and to be ready. And Sheriff, call animal control and have them pick up that dead squirrel so it can be checked for any diseases!”

Doctor Spellman, was a Specialist in Disease Control and had been notified of the situation. He called over to the Animal Control Center and left instructions with Jacob, the local veterinarian. “Extract any blood samples you can from the squirrel and have it tested immediately for rabies or the plague." "The plague?" "Yes, the fucking plague and do it now!"

Just then Ronda, TJ's mother, Sharon, Miko and the children arrived. Sharon was the first one out of the car. "Where is my son? Is he ok?" Hank pulled up right behind them and motioned to some nurses that the boy was in the back seat. They put him on the gurney and began checking his vital signs. Spellman explained to TJ's mother about the possibility of infection. He asked her to try to be calm and then disappeared into one of the operating rooms with his team.

"Ronda come with me," Miko directed, heading towards the elevators. "What?" Ronda seemed surprised. "What about the kids?" "Tell Hank to keep an eye on them, just come on." Miko ducked down an empty hallway and the next thing Ronda knew she was on an elevator to the sixth floor. "Miko where are we going?" "You have to see this," Miko explained. "Did you tell Hank what I found?" "Shit," Ronda said—"after the kids came running in, I didn't get a chance to finish telling him." "What was wrong with them anyway?" Miko asked. Ronda hadn't had a chance to explain about the hand the girls found. "A hand fell out of a tree at the park." "What!" Miko screamed, at that moment the elevator stopped on six. "What the fuck is going on?" As they approached Lab 612, Miko thought she heard that gnawing sound again. "Do you hear that Ronda?" Miko asked. At that point she had the door open, she left the flashlight in her purse so she could see. She shined the light to the back of the lab and said, "You see, look." The fetuses Ronda saw in the jar almost made her gag. "Why would they keep unborn fetuses up here?" The thought of what they might be doing with them was disheartening, they both thought to themselves. They were labeled in terms of age. One week. Two weeks. Three months. Six months. Nine months. "Let's go." Ronda had seen enough. Trembling now, she grabbed Miko and headed for the door. There it was again that gnawing sound, only this time it was louder. "Miko, let's go," she whispered. "No," said Miko, "I have to see what that is." "Are you out of your mind, I'm not going in there, don't you hear that?" "Yes, that's why I have to see what it is; I won't have another chance." "Fuck that shit," said Ronda. "Then stay here." "Fuck that too. Come on—just hurry."

Downstairs Terrez was explaining to TJ's mother and Hank just what had happened. "Why, why would you kids be in the ravines shooting at anything, why were you down there period?" She was screaming and crying hysterically.

In the operating room Spellman gave TJ all the necessary vaccinations and put him on life support machines. He prayed that TJ didn't have the plague which ground squirrels are common hosts of. He treated him with antibiotics just in case.

Miko and Ronda were at Lab 621. Miko was fumbling with the keys again. Fat Lou was also on the sixth floor he had been trying to get into Lab 621 and was unable to, so he went down another hallway when he heard what he thought were voices whispering. Miko was just about to open the door when she felt a hand on her shoulder and a voice say, "What's going on up here?" "Who the hell are you?" Ronda screamed. Miko turned and hit Fat Lou across the face with her flashlight and pushed him to the ground. She grabbed Ronda and they darted for the stairs. Lou got himself up and looked bewildered, "Who was that? And what were they doing up here?" Then he heard it—the gnawing sound was coming from the lab he now stood right in front of. His first thought was to leave but he thought about Dr. Going, so he reached his hand down and slowly turned the doorknob to Lab 621—the gnawing stopped.

Miko and Ronda burst through the stairwell door on the first floor slamming it into Dr. Spellman. He was just about to ask them what they were doing coming from that door because that stairway led up to the sixth floor; when Sharon, Hank and Sheriff Brown walked up. The Sheriff had just arrived. He got a call from one of his deputies, in route to the hospital, about an abandon car on Route 99. This peeked his curiosity because hardly anyone in town used that route any more. The doctors and lawyers of Sherfield community along with the Mayor and the City Council had petitioned and succeeded in re-zoning that route. Noise pollution was something that the residents of Somerset Street refused to tolerate from the highway known as Route 99, which was directly behind them.

Fat Lou's flashlight was running low and he couldn't see the small black beady-eyed figures staring at him from all over the lab. He started to hear little taps running across the floors and shelves. He felt something run up his pants leg and the flashlight came back on. Then he felt the sharp incisor teeth pierce his nuts. He puked blood from his mouth, saw something fly towards him and felt the sharp incisor teeth strike again. This time the powerful jaws crush his nuts and what seemed to be hundreds of the little flying animals started tearing him apart.

Dr. Spellman entered the waiting room where Sharon was crying hysterically. "How is he? Is he going to be alright? Can I see him?" "He's in a state of shock but that's to be expected seeing what he just went though. We took some blood and we're having it tested." "Tested for what?" "Well a squirrel bit him so it's normal procedure. Right now he's stable and resting. I gave him something to help him sleep and take his mind off the trauma. Now why don't you go home and try to get some rest." "I could never leave my son, I'll be right here. When I leave TJ leaves with me." Sheriff Brown informed Hank about the accident on Route 99 and told him he'd like to speak with him first thing in the morning. All the children were asleep now. Ronda and Miko needed to tell Hank what they had found. After they arrived at the house Ronda bedded the children down. Hank poured himself and Miko a drink. Then the two women told Hank about the terrifying discovery they found on the sixth floor of Newton General Hospital.

That Sunday morning, JP called around six o' clock, everyone else was still asleep. She told Hank about the racket from last night and how she had not checked to see what happened. "I'll be there in about a hour and JP, the Sheriff will be with me." "I have to meet him anyway so you might as well let him take a look." Hank showered then phoned the Sheriff and told him to meet him over JP's. He told Ronda where he was going, gave her a kiss and told her not to let the kids go pass the front of the house or the backyard. Miko and Shannon had spent the night. Everyone else in the house was still asleep when Hank left.

As he pulled up he could see Sheriff Brown sitting in the driveway. "Good morning Sheriff," Hank said as he walked up to him. "Let's hope so," he replied. JP had seen them walking up and opened the front door; she hadn't heard Red-Dog barking which he always did whenever someone approached the house. "What happened Ms. Peterson?" the Sheriff asked. She explained to the two men how after she returned from the party the noises started and something or someone had been in the yard. "Ok, lets take a look," Sheriff Brown motioned to Hank. As the two men looked around the back yard they saw Red-Dog with blood all over his face and what appeared to be bite marks and scratches. Red-Dog just laid still watching the two men apparently tired and injured from his battle the night before, but with what?

Then Hank spoke, "Over here." What they saw looked to be a small animal that had been torn apart in the battle, blood and guts were all over the lawn. Crows were circling the area and had been picking at the dead carcass. "Let me get animal control over here to remove this mess and do some tests to see just what this piece of shit was. You will definitely want to get your dog checked out in case he has rabies; whatever he was fighting looks like it got a couple good licks on him too." Hank asked JP if she was going to be all right, she told him she would be fine but to just call and check on her later. The Sheriff made the call. Animal Control would come and clean up the mess and take the remains of whatever lay scattered all over the yard back to the lab for testing. They would also take Red-Dog. With that, the Sheriff asked Hank if he would like to go out to Route 99 with him. Hank said he would and asked the Sheriff about TJ. "He's unchanged at the moment, Sharon will call me and let me know if there's any change." "I would just like to tell you how sorry I am," Hank was telling the Sheriff. "It's not your fault how could anyone have known or have suspected a squirrel would attach anyone."

As they approached the scene of the accident they could see the deputies had closed the area off. There was a Ford Explorer overturned in a ditch. Glass was all over the tree-lined highway. "Blowout?" The Sheriff asked the deputy. "No, you need to take a look at this it's the damn dist thing I've ever seen," the deputy replied.

Chapter 9

Forest Chapman was an intern doctor at Newton General, who studied under the guidance of Dr. Josh Jackson. Chapman, who knew Jackson was doing unethical experiments on the sixth floor, had threatened to expose Jackson if he did not cease to conduct his gross regeneration efforts. He was banned from practicing medicine in Newton County in 1991. Dr. Going a colleague of Jackson's in the early 1970's and the Chief of Operations at Newton saw to that. He was forced to move to Aspen, Iowa and practice medicine at Bedford County Hospital, or never practice medicine again. It was at that time a young Michigan doctor named Lou Spellman, worked at Bedford.

Dr. Lou Spellman, was a foster child who had been raised by a single woman simply called Aunti, who ran a home day care center in Ferndale, Michigan. As a medical student at the University of Michigan, Spellman, often wondered how she could afford his tuition. When he asked about his biological parents she told him they were killed in a plane crash while traveling out the country. While searching through some old relics in the basement, he'd come across many pictures of a couple that seemed to be in a remote area. On the back of the pictures was always the note: Please Give Him Our Love.

After obtaining his degree Spellman moved to Iowa. Doctors were in heavy demand there and research grants were easy to obtain in that state. He heard of Dr. Jackson's work and decided to go into the field of Genetic Engineering and Disease Control. Spellman took the pictures of the young couple and one day Chapman, while browsing through Spellman's office came across the picture of a young Dr. Jackson. Chapman had heard stories that Dr. Jackson and Professor Straub had a child while doing research in Asia and sent the child back to the States to protect it from the plague, which had spread across southern Asia in the seventies. He shared this information with Spellman and told him how he had been kicked out of

Newton. Between Jackson and Going, the two devised a plan to try and find out about the truth of the Asian experiments.

Afterwards, Spellman transferred to Newton General and moved into Jackson's old home. He made some shocking discoveries. He had been in constant contact with Chapman and the two knew they were close to finding out the truth. Chapman decided it would be best for him to take a leave of absence from the job and return to Newton. He would stay at the house with Spellman. While driving down Route 99 about five miles from Newton, Chapman ran over some type of animal in the road. "Shit, what the hell was that," he said, to himself. Chapman got out of the car on the dark lonely highway to investigate. At that moment, something swooped out of the trees and landed right on his face. The animal started gnawing at his lip. Chapman screamed and snatched the small creature off. He ran towards the car and was attacked by several more of the animals that flew out of the trees. He fell to the ground, the sharp incisor bites were taking their toll on him and he knew he had to get back to the car. With one last painful effort he snatched the creatures off him and raced to the car.

Bloody and shaken he peeled off, sped down the highway when one jumped out from the rear seat onto the back of his neck. He grabbed the animal, rolled down his window and tossed it out of the car. Two more crashed into the windshield then he could feel them all over his legs, they were in the car. He screamed as they bit him over and over again. At that point, he lost control of the SUV and it flipped over and over until it came to rest in a lonely ditch. His hand was severed from his body and right before he died he saw one of the flying squirrels fly off. His last thought was, my God it can't be here, that's impossible.

Sheriff Brown and Hank were at the car now and Hank gagged at the awful sight of what used to be a man. He had been picked down to the bone. The crows were still feeding on pieces of the man further up the highway. That's when they saw it, what looked like a dead squirrel with wings in the back seat. Both men noticed the missing hand and at the same time reached for their cell phones. The deputy handed Sheriff Brown a wallet. As he looked in the wallet he was startled to see the name of, Dr. Lou Spellman. "Shit," he said out loud. Sharon answered the phone and the Sheriff asked her about TJ. "There's been no change," she told him. "I'm worried." "We all are, we just have to stay strong and pray." "Have you seen Dr. Spellman?" he asked. "No, why what's wrong?" Sharon replied. "It's nothing, I just need to ask him a couple of questions."

Hank was having no luck getting through to his house, those kids must have the phone tied up, "damn," he shouted.

Chapter 10

(Flashback)

For the next three months Josh and Lisa stayed very close making preparations for the trip to Asia. Lisa was pregnant but she was afraid Josh wouldn't approve so she decided to wait until they were in Asia to tell him. Lisa had received her grant from the private sector. A billionaire by the name of Hughes who's son had been born with congenital disorders due to his wife taking the sedative thalidomide, which had not been approved in the States. He'd hoped her research would bring a cure to his only son. His wife had committed suicide after the child was born. Lisa had not told Josh and knew he didn't care about where the money came from. When they arrived in Asia their working facilities were set and ready to go. Josh had smuggled some ground squirrels into the country because they were not common there. He had also brought some fetuses for his cloning experiments. Josh would often use the people in the nearby village for some of his experiments. Many of the women he drew cells from had been exposed to external factors such as too much heat and different infectious agents. Many of the clones he produced were called Teratogen. The research was going terrible. Lisa was pregnant, not to mention the plague was sweeping across southern Asia. They both agreed that as soon as the baby was born they would send it back to the States with Lisa's sister who ran a day care center in Michigan. Lisa's early hybridization experiments with the three different squirrel breeds were also producing monstrous results. They spent the next seventeen years there. Then, sometime around 1991, they returned to the States because Lisa had gotten very ill and Josh did not have the proper medicine or facilities to care for her. He contacted his old colleague Dr. Goings in Iowa, and the two made preparations for the couple's return.

Chapter 11

Jacob had just finished with his diagnosis of the hand when the rest of the crew came in from JP's house with Red-Dog and the remains of whatever they had scraped off the lawn. He detected two different saliva types from the hand. One was a ground squirrel and the other was a flying squirrel. It didn't make any sense; flying squirrels were rare in North America, especially in these parts. He observed something else too, it seemed that the flying squirrel's saliva had been mutated or crossbred with something else. He called the Sheriff and then called a friend of his in Atlanta and told her he was sending the samples via Airborne Express. "Here, let's test this pooch for rabies," Jacob instructed the other men.

Shortly after Jacob completed the test Sheriff Brown and Hank arrived. “Hope you have some good news for us, Jacob,” Sheriff Brown said. “Sorry, it’s far from good news, we may have a little disaster here in Newton,” he began to explain to the men. “According to the samples I took, this hand was bitten by some type of rodent in the Sciuridae family that somehow became mutated or a victim of hybridization.” Hank cut in shouting, “What the fuck are you talking about, speak English!” “Sorry,” Jacob said, “the fact of the matter is, this hand was bitten by a cross breed of squirrels. I believe it was a mix of a ground squirrel and a flying squirrel.” “Are you sure about this?” the Sheriff asked. “Ninety percent sure, sir. But wait there’s more. Another bite mark appeared to have a third type of the species. My guess is the tree squirrel. I sent the samples to Atlanta for a second opinion, I should know more tomorrow. I also notified Dr. Spellman.” “Spellman, when? And where is he?” the Sheriff asked. “He was at his home,” Jacob replied. “Mr. Peterson, I have some more bad news. Your mother’s dog has rabies; he apparently was fighting with one of these mutated squirrels. He’s going to have to be put to sleep.” “Are you kidding?” “No,” Jacob said. “There is no cure for rabies in animals.” “Well, we found a dead squirrel at the accident that looked like it had wings of some sort. They’re bringing it over to you so find out what the hell is going on and call me right away, and don’t tell Spellman shit else until I’ve talked to him, is that clear Jacob?” “Yes, yes of course, Sheriff.”

Chapter 12

Lou Spellman had gotten Jacob's call and feared the worst. He was beginning to worry now about TJ, he had not heard from Dr. Chapman, who should have made it into town by now; but there were no messages at his home or the hospital. He'd left the hospital a couple of hours ago to come home and freshen up. Then he remembered the two women coming from the stairwell. One, he thought he had seen before but couldn't put his finger on it. What could they have been doing up there? All the other floor entrances were sealed off. You had to already be on six to exit this way. In his own basement he had uncovered some of Josh and Lisa's research notes. They had come very close to uncovering the secret of regeneration in humans. He had also discovered a hidden door. The door had remained locked until a couple of months ago when he found a strange old key, he'd tried the key and it worked. Once he opened the door strange blinking lights started flashing and would not shut off until the door was closed. It appeared to lead down a long hallway, to what he wasn't sure but he was too afraid to continue any further.

Dr. Spellman decided he had better get back to the hospital and make his rounds, check on TJ and try to find out what those two women were doing coming out of the stairway from six. Then it struck him where he had seen one of the women before. It was Miko she worked at the hospital, "Damn it," he thought as he locked his door and headed for his car in the driveway.

Chapter 13

At the Peterson's house the girls were in the backyard all except for Tash, she was in the basement with Terrez watching cartoons. Ronda and Miko were in the family room discussing yesterday's chain of events and what could possibly be in Lab 621. That's when Jasmine came into the house and asked if they could sit in the jeep and listen to her CD Destiny's Child. Her mother told her yes, but not to blast it. Jasmine grabbed the CD and ran into the backyard. "Come on y'all"—she said, "yes!" They ran and got into the jeep, Jasmine sat in the driver's seat, Porter next to her and Shannon behind Porter. The girls were teasing Shannon and Jasmine was laughing about how she had thrown up the cookies and milk. But Shannon was telling Porter that she didn't even see the hand—when Porter looked out of the window and shouted, "Look, did you see that?" "See what?" Jasmine asked. "It looked like I just saw a squirrel fly onto the roof of the house." Jasmine started laughing loudly and said, "yeah—right girl, sure you did; but you know that squirrels can't fly." "No, look," Shannon said, "I saw it too, see up on the roof?" "Those are birds, y'all are tripping." None of the girls noticed the squirrels in the trees above them. "I'm scared, let's go back in the house."

Miko got up from the couch to go look out the front door, when the phone rang. It was Hank. "Ronda, where are the kids?" "Terrez and Tash are in the basement, the rest of the girls are in the jeep." Shannon opened the door to the jeep and the girls were walking towards the house when about three squirrels flew off the roof and headed right for them. The girls started screaming and running for the house; Shannon fell and one of the squirrels landed on her back, by that time the other squirrels were swooping down at the girls.

Miko screamed, grabbed a broom and ran out the front door swinging the broom at the squirrels. She knocked the squirrel off Shannon's back, picked her up and dragged her into the house. Ronda had dropped the phone and was screaming. Jasmine and Porter ran and hopped back into the jeep. The squirrels in the tree were dropping on the roof of the jeep and gnawing wildly trying to get to the girls. Hank was on the phone shouting for Ronda. Terrez and Tash were looking out the front window.

Miko managed to get Shannon in the house and was ripping off her clothes, which had blood on them. "Did they bite you?" she shouted. Shannon was crying. She asked again, "Did they bite you?" "No, I don't think so," the girl sobbed. "Ronda, get me some clothes." Ronda was about to open the front door and try to get the two other girls out of the jeep when Miko grabbed her and said, "No, Ronda, No you can't go out there, they'll get you too." "But I have to get my baby," Ronda shouted. "Not now—they're safe for now, those things can't get in as long as they keep the doors and windows locked." Hank was on the phone still shouting when Ronda picked it back up. "What happened? he asked." Ronda tried to explain but was shaken up too badly. "I'll be there in ten minutes," Hank said and hung up the phone. "I have to get to my house now," he told the Sheriff. "There's been another attack."

The two men had been in route to Dr. Spellman's house when Hank got through, so they were not far away.

Sheriff Brown had just turned onto Somerset Street and came to a screeching stop in front of Dr. Spellman's house. He was in shock at the carving of the giant squirrel that sat out in front. "What kind of fucked up decoration was this? Just what was going on here and what was the doctor up to?" He pulled his gun as he rang the front doorbell, no answer. He slowly crept around the house checking doors and windows for a way in but everything was locked.

Spellman had received a page from the hospital and hurried to get back there. When he arrived the nurses and TJ's mom were in the room with TJ, his vital signs were low and he was sweating terribly. Suddenly he started shaking and spitting up blood, his head was turning from side to side. "Hold him," Spellman shouted. "TJ!" his mother screamed. "Get her out of here and get me that spoon!" He shoved the spoon down TJ's mouth and gave him a shot to calm him down. A few minutes later, Spellman came out of the room and told TJ's mom, that TJ was stable and was just reacting to the medication.

The sheriff not being able to get into the house, got in his car and drove away and decided to check in on Jacob on his way back to the hospital. His radio went off, it was an emergency 911 from the Peterson's house. "What now?" he thought to himself, putting on the siren and speeding that way, he called Hank.

Hank had arrived and to his dismay saw the squirrels trying to get into the jeep. He blew his horn, flashed his lights and smashed right into the jeep. The impact scared the squirrels away. He took the girls inside and the whole family remained there. Sheriff Brown had just arrived and came in through the front door. Shannon was asleep and the rest of the kids were in the basement talking about what had happened. Miko offered the Sheriff a drink and he accepted. The four of them sat down in the living room and the ladies told their story; then Hank and the Sheriff told theirs. They all agreed that Spellman was linked to or knew something about what was going on. The Sheriff posted a deputy in the house with the Peterson family and asked Hank to ride with him. "Be careful," Ronda exclaimed as she gave Hank a big hug and a long wet kiss. The kids all gave him big hugs too. Miko wanted to hug the Sheriff but instead told them to be careful and keep the lines open. Hank knew that with the deputy and Miko there, the family would be safe. Ronda's sister didn't take shit from anyone or anything, he thought to himself.

Sheriff Brown called back to the hospital to try and reach Spellman but was told he would be in surgery for the next three or four hours. The Sheriff also called the Mayor to get a search warrant for Spellman's house and had not heard back from him yet. The Mayor was also the local judge in town. "We have to get back to Jacob to see if he's found out anything else," the Sheriff was explaining to Hank as he sped down the road.

Chapter 14

Jacob's samples arrived in Atlanta at the Center for Disease Control about an hour earlier. The package was addressed to: Ms. Renee Ward. Renee Ward was a beautiful brown-skinned black woman with medium breasts, braids in her hair and light brown eyes. She had obtained a degree in biotechnology at the University of Washington. Afterwards, she worked at the Center for Disease Control (CDC) in Spokane, Washington. Renee was well known for her brief stints in quarantines and working in the Public Health Practice Program Office (PHPPO).

Renee was a single woman with no children and hadn't really been seriously involved in a relationship in the last couple of years, although she had dated a few married men. She thought that was easier because they always had to go home to their wives and children. It worked out because of her long working hours and traveling.

Bear Russell, was the current Director of the (CDC) in Atlanta, Georgia and the CDC was an agency of the Department of Health and Human Services. Two years ago after a CDC convention in Boston, Bear had offered Renee the job of the Assistant Director of the Epidemiologist Program Office (EPO).

Renee and Jacob had met at the convention and became friends. It was about six thirty when the samples arrived at the CDC in Atlanta. She could tell there was some sort of serious problem in Newton by the sound of Jacob's voice and by what he had described over the phone. She'd already spoken to the Director and was awaiting the samples.

Chapter 15

At Newton General, Dr. Going had received a call from his sister Katie. She was worried because her husband fat Lou hadn't come home last night. "He's probably somewhere drunk, Katie," Going was saying. "Bullshit," she said, "he always at least comes home and why do you have to treat him so badly? Could you at least help me find him for God's sake? You know how hard you ride him." Going loved his sister and couldn't understand why she was with this fat slob, but he had helped her get the contract for Klean & Klean and didn't want to upset her so he told her he would check into it. "Please do, Steve, please for me." "All right Katie, I will, I promise." Dr. Steve Going hated the fact that his only sister was with this loser but he had promised to take care of her when their parents had died a long time ago. Going called his secretary and asked her to have Mike come to his office.

Mike was getting nervous now he had tried to call Miko but only gotten her voicemail at home. He needed to be sure no one knew about the keys he'd stolen and given her but he couldn't wait—you didn't make Going's wait because if you did you would be out of a job. The word had always been around about how he had gotten rid of some of his top doctors—so what chance did anyone else have? This was the question always asked around the hospital. Mike was sitting down outside of Dr. Going's office when his secretary told him he could go in. He walked in and Going motioned for him to have a seat, he was on the phone. "Mike, how are you?" Going asked. "Just fine, Dr. Going, what can I do for you?" "Mike, I'll get straight to the point. Have you seen Lou today?"

Chapter 16

It was about 2:30 when Hank and the Sheriff arrived at the Vet. Jacob told them Renee Ward would be there soon. The decomposed body of Dr. Chapman had arrived and the three of them were ready to take another look but Renee had told Jacob to wait until she got there. "Just who is this Renee Ward and why do we need outside help?" the Sheriff asked Jacob. He explained her background to the men and informed the Sheriff that Newton might have an epidemic on their hands if they didn't get her and her equipment in here ASAP. Newton just didn't have the right facilities for the test he needed to run to be sure. "Sure of what? What kind of epidemic are you talking about?" Hank asked. Jacob had not told the two men about Dr. Spellman's mention of the Plague and he was not an expert in diseases so he tried to shrug off the question. Sheriff Brown repeated the question. "What kind of epidemic are you talking about Jacob? I need some answers and I need them right now." At that moment a soft voice cut in and said, "The Plague, gentlemen; he's talking about the Plague." The three men turned around to see a very attractive young Black woman with braids in her hair, standing with two men beside her. "Renee," Jacob said, "how are you? You look great!" "I'm fine, been better but how are you? It's been awhile since I saw you last. Anyway let me introduce you to my guys. This is Sam Johnson and Dave Dysan. They work for me down at the Center." "Nice to meet you both. This is Sheriff Tyrone Brown and Hank Peterson, one of our local businessmen here in Newton." "Nice to meet you all, but what is this I hear you saying about a Plague?" the Sheriff asked. "Just a minute Sheriff," Renee said. "Sam, bring the stuff in. Where can we set up Jacob?" "Right in here" he replied. Dave and Sam went outside to the van and started unloading boxes of equipment. Renee began to explain. "Based on the samples you sent me you were right they were squirrel bites. But these bites are from three different types of squirrels; these squirrels have been crossbred." "Crossbred? What exactly are you saying?" Hank asked. "I'm saying that someone had crossbred some squirrels somewhere and what you have is a clone of all three types of squirrels. If you didn't know, ground squirrels carry the Plague. I'm almost certain it's going to spread. Now let's have a look at that body. In the meantime, we may need to seal off the town." "Hold on just a minute the Sheriff said. Just who the Hell do you think you are? You can't come in here talking of sealing off the town, you have no jurisdiction here." "Sheriff Brown, I am the Assistant Director of the CDC, which is an agency of the U.S. Department of Health and Human Services and that gives me the entire goddamn jurisdiction I need. But what I don't have time for is to get into a pissing contest with the locals in charge here. So what I need you to do is contact whomever you need to and get them on the phone and tell them the town is on possible alert to be sealed off. I will let you know just as soon as I finish looking at this body if it's necessary." "Fine," the Sheriff said. "Hank I'm going to head over to the Mayor's office, I have to pick up something from him anyway. Jacob, call me just as soon as you find out something." "Ok" Jacob said. With that he and Renee went into the lab on the other side of the vet's office that was sometimes used as a mini morgue. Hank decided to stay at the vet's office, he told the Sheriff he would catch up with him later.

Hank watched Renee start her test on the body. "Is someone going to fill me in on what happen here or are you going to just stand there and stare? Maybe you didn't hear me out there but it's a good chance that this town is about to be hit with the plague, and please start at the beginning and don't leave anything out." "Ok, this is what I know." He explained about the kids, the B-B gun, how the squirrel had bitten TJ and how he had killed it. "Where is the boy now?" Renee asked. "At Newton General," Hank answered. Then Renee asked if the good doctor had started anyone on Streptomycin or Tetracycline. "What?" Hank asked. "Antibiotics," Jacob and Renee both said. "No," Hank replied. "Damn him, ok we have to get to your family and everyone you have come in contact with in the past 24 hours. In fact, this body has signs of the plague all over it. This town is going to have to be sealed off. I brought a couple of cases with me so I can start you two on the antibiotics now. Dave and Sam will help you dispose of this body and sanitize this place. Also, call the Sheriff, get him back here ASAP and his deputies. Jacob and I need to look at these animal carcass now." Renee was a very direct woman Hank could see that and he had no time to argue about things he didn't know about.

"Mr. Peterson, we need to get to your house fast. We can take my van." She instructed Dave and Sam on what to do and the two of them walked out to the van. "If you hear from Spellman, tell him nothing, I've got a feeling something's going on in this town and he may be a part of it." The two of them got into the van and drove off. But what they didn't see was all the squirrels in the trees and on the roof of the building.

Chapter 17

Mike had just got up to the sixth floor, "Damn something up here smells bad." It was then he heard the gnawing sound coming from Lab 621. He headed for the lab when he was hit from behind and knocked unconscious. Dr. Spellman was also on that floor and had heard Mike coming up the stairs. Now, who was up here? And why? He dragged Mike to one of the empty labs, injected him with some type of drug that would keep him out for at least ten to twelve hours. Then Spellman tied and gagged him; it was at that moment he heard his name on the intercom—Dr. Spellman, please report to Dr. Going's office. He was shocked, what could Going want with him. He went to Going's office and the secretary motioned for him to have a seat—"He'll be with you in a moment." Going was finishing a call. Then he stuck his head out the office and called Spellman in. "Come in, Doctor, please come in and have a seat." Spellman sat down and waited for Going to tell him what the meeting was all about. Then Going spoke, "Dr. Spellman, you just recently transferred here from Bedford, is that correct?" "Yes sir," Spellman answered, still wondering what was going on. "And you did your schooling in Michigan, correct?" Again, Spellman answered "yes." "I'm sorry, would you care for some coffee, tea, or a drink?" "No thank you sir, but if we could get to the point, I have a patient that I need to check on." "Would that patient be the little boy that was bitten by the squirrel, Dr. Spellman?" "Yes sir, it would be," Spellman replied. "Doctor has the boy been checked for the Plague and treated?" "Yes sir, he has all the symptoms of bubonic plague, his lymph nodes of the groin and neck are very swollen. His temperature is at 39.3 C and 103 F. His pulse and respiration rate has also increased. Due to the fact that he's still in a state of shock and unable to speak to us; I have him on life support and in isolation. We're treating him with antibiotics." "Well doctor, why wasn't this brought to my attention and what's the chance of this spreading? Surely you know the proper procedures in a case like this?" "Yes sir, I've been meaning to notify you personally but the report was submitted this morning." "This morning, you say?" "Yes sir, this morning and again I do have him in isolation to prevent the disease from spreading." Going poured himself a drink and then spoke again. "I understand you moved into the house on Somerset Street?" "Yes, but what does that have to do with any of this?" Spellman asked. "Well, it's just that an old friend of mine use to live there years ago. As a matter of fact you may have heard of him, he worked here." Now Spellman was really confused and wanted to know where this was going. Then Going asked him, "Have you had lunch yet?" "No sir, but I really need to check on the boy if you don't mind." "Yes, I do mind. We'll get someone else to check on him. We need to talk so get your things and let's go get a bite to eat and I'll explain what this is all about. I know this nice little Deli where we can talk. Meet me in the front in ten minutes, I'll drive," Going instructed him. The two men met in front and headed for the Deli.

Chapter 18

Sheriff Brown had arrived at Newton's Municipal Office where the Mayor/Judge was located; the Mayor was a young white ambitious man in his mid-thirties who had obtained a Master's degree in Government and was at the top of his class on the bar exam. He also held a degree in Business Administration. He had a plush office on the tenth floor and a beautiful young secretary who he'd screw occasionally all over the office. He was still single and often had young ladies in his office for a brief fling. Sheriff Brown had called and told the Mayor/Judge he needed to speak to him right away; so when he got there Mayor Ronald Nelson was waiting.

Sandra, the young secretary told him to go right in. "Tyrone," the Mayor said. "How are you? What can I do for you today?" "Well, Ron," the Sheriff said, "we may have a bit of a problem." The two men were on a first name basis for now. "Grab a seat." "What problem could we possibly have on a fine summer day like this?" "Well Ron, I don't know if you heard but yesterday one of the local boys was attacked by a squirrel." "Did I just hear you right, Ty? Attacked by a squirrel?" "Yes, you heard me right." "Hold on here, squirrels don't attack people—people attack people, dogs attack people. I have never in my life heard of a fucking squirrel attacking anyone. And if it did there must have been a good—real good reason for it. Now I'm a busy man what is this all about, Tyrone?" "Well, some kids were down in the ravines shooting a B-B gun at some squirrels and trapped one and it lashed out and bit one of them." "Well then, there you have it; they were the real attackers, my good man." "No, there's more, apparently squirrels can carry the Plague. There was another attack on Route 99 and we've got a dead body. We also have a local woman, one of your best supporters; whose dog had a fight with one of these squirrels and now it has to be put to sleep." The Mayor/Judge was now giving the Sheriff his full attention. "We also found a dead squirrel with what looked like wings of some sort at the scene of the dead body. Jacob called in a woman from the CDC in Atlanta and she wants to seal off the town in case we are hit with the Plague. Now some kind of way, Dr. Lou Spellman, from Newton General is connected. I went out to his house and what does he have in his front yard?—A tree carving of a squirrel in front. What I need from you is a search warrant to have a look inside his house." "Hold the fuck on for a minute here Sheriff! First of all I run this fucking town and no goddamn skirt from Atlanta or anywhere else is going to seal off my town and cause an unwarranted panic because of what appears to be a couple of accidents. Do I need to remind you that the County Fair is in two days? As you well know the fair brings in fifty percent of this town's yearly revenue. And there is no way in hell I'm going to give you a search warrant because someone has a tree carving in front of their home. Listen to yourself man, are you fucking crazy or don't you remember how important the fair is to this town or don't you remember that you are up for re-election in six months? Has anyone at Newton General contacted you? Did they make the call and bring in this bitch from Atlanta who knows nothing about our way of living?" Tyrone felt a lump in his throat. "Well, did they Sheriff Brown?" "No, but…" "Fuck but, that's what you do with it and until you can get me more facts than this bullshit you just came in here with, you remember who runs this fucking town. Now as I said, I'm a busy man, get out!" The Sheriff got up and left. Then the Mayor called Sandra in and got real busy with a head job.

Sheriff Brown was disgusted now and felt a headache coming on. Little did he know, this was the first symptom of the Plague. He stopped at the local drug store, picked up some aspirin, then decided to go by the hospital and catch up with Dr. Spellman. By the time he got there he had just missed Spellman and Going. He went to the front desk and asked the nurse if Spellman was there. "No, he just left with Dr. Going, they were going out for lunch." Suddenly, the Sheriff felt like he had to vomit and started to cough violently. The nurse asked if he was ok and he just nodded his head "yes" and walked out of the hospital. "Did you just see that?" the nurse asked the other nurse as she wiped the fluids off her face from his coughing. "Nasty, germy mother-fucker. That's why I hate working here—all these sick mother-fuckers."

The nurse had given the Sheriff, Dr. Spellman's cell phone number and he decided to give him a call. The doctor's phone rang, he said, excuse me to Going and answered. "Dr. Spellman here." "Hello, Dr. Spellman, this is Sheriff Brown. I just left the hospital and the nurse gave me your number. Doctor I understand you and Dr. Going are headed for the deli?" "Yes, Sheriff that's true. We're about to have lunch." Going was looking and listening as he drove towards the deli. "Well, Doctor, I need about ten minutes of your time, I have a few questions I need you to answer for me and I was just going to meet you there." "Excuse me Sheriff, but right now is not a very good time. As you already said I'm having lunch with my boss and it's private." "Well sir," the Sheriff said, "this will not wait any longer so I'll see you at the deli" and he hung up. "Bastard," Spellman said. "Is everything all right Dr. Spellman?" Going asked. "Yes sir, and I have to apologize that was the Sheriff; he needs me to clear something up for him so he's going to come by the deli. I hope you don't mind." "No, not at all," Dr. Going said. "Let's see exactly what the good Sheriff wants." Spellman was confused and bewildered but had no choice but to see what the Doctor and the Sheriff wanted from him. Then he remembered he still had not heard from Chapman. Could this all be related he thought to himself as they pulled up to the valet parking at the deli.

The two men went inside and one of the waitresses seated them in the non-smoking section and asked if they would like a cocktail before they ordered. Going ordered a martini and Spellman ordered a double scotch. Just when the young pretty waitress was bringing the two their drinks, the Sheriff walked in. He spotted the men and headed in their direction. When he got to the table the waitress asked if he would like a menu or if he would like to order a drink. "No thanks," he said. "I'm still on duty." He noticed the Doctors had ordered drinks and thought to himself, "this is why they got so many lawsuits against them, they were fucking drunks." He sat down across from Spellman and next to Going. "Doctor, how's TJ doing?" "The boy is doing fine, Sheriff but I doubt you came all the way here for that; so if you could just get to the point," Spellman replied. "Of course, I can see you two are very busy. Doctor last night there was an accident on Route 99 not too far from your house and a man was killed." "Well, I'm sorry to hear that Sheriff. But what has that got to do with me?" "Well, do you know a Dr. Forest Chapman from Bedford Hospital?" Going broke out in a sweat when he heard the name. Dr. Spellman lied and said he'd never heard of him. "Are you sure doctor?" the Sheriff asked. "Well, Sheriff I know a lot of doctors and I did use to work at Bedford but I still don't recall a Chatman." "No, I said Chapman," the Sheriff said. "Whoever," Spellman blurted out. "I said I don't know him, now if you would please, we'd like to order our lunch and your ten minutes are up Sheriff." "Of course, of course." The Sheriff stood up and said, "Sorry to have bothered you, gentleman." He started to walk away then turned around and said, "You know Dr. Spellman there's just one thing that bothers me. You say you don't know of the late doctor but I have a feeling he knew of you because we found this card with your name and address and the time ten o' clock in his wallet. I'll be in touch with you Doctor." Then the Sheriff walked out.

Chapter 19

Jacob, Dave, and Sam had opened all the windows and doors on the morgue side of the building. They would sanitize it first because of the powerful chemicals and fumes. They didn't want the few animals on the other side of the building to get any sicker than they already were. "Let's start in the back and work our way forward," Sam suggested. Dave and Jacob both agreed and the three men took all of the materials to the back room. They had already cremated Dr. Chapman, Red-Dog and the squirrel carcass. So now it was just a point of decontaminating the place.

That's when Sam heard the gnawing and what seem to be like little paw sounds running across the floor in the front room. "Quiet," he said. "Did you hear that?" "Yes," both men nodded. "I'd better check it out, cut off that radio. Dave, get your gun, I don't like the sound of this. Jacob, go in the next room and start closing those windows and doors." "Okay," Jacob said, and left out of the room. He turned to the left and was headed to the back when he heard Sam scream.

Sam walked to the front of the building when he saw the squirrels all over the place. They were leaping through the windows, flying through the door and biting him all over. One had pierced his eye with a single bite and blood was gushing everywhere; the flying ones had covered the whole topside of his body and were ripping him apart in chunks. The others had brought him down. The screaming was loud and fierce until they ate his vocal chords out and continued to feast on the body. Jacob started running and the flying squirrels were now on his back biting him on the back of the neck. He snatched them off and smashed them against the walls. Others he slammed to the floor and stomped to death but there were too many of them. He heard shots coming from the other room but the pain of the squirrels ripping him apart was too much and he fell helplessly to the floor. Jacob didn't die right away; he felt every chunk of flesh being pulled from his body. The squirrels ripped him down to the bone, feeding on every one of his body organs until there was nothing left. What was left of Jacob lie in a puddle of blood that spread outside his skeleton.

Dave was being attacked in the other room. He was shooting wildly, only hitting a few of them. The ground squirrels had proven to be too much for Dave. He could see the flying squirrels now, flying into the room and he just couldn't bear the thought of being eaten alive so he put the gun to his head and shouted, "Fuck you," before he blew his brains all over the room. The squirrels feasted on his remains and left the building in what appeared to be an army.

Renee and Hank were in the van heading for his house when she noticed he was really kind of cute and also had cute dimples. Then she asked him just what he did for a living. "I own a couple of car dealerships here in town. In fact, that's what brought me here." "That was going to be my next question," she said with a smooth tone. "I really was wondering what a city guy like you was doing out here in Newton, Iowa?" "Is it that obvious?" "Of course, it is."

"I mean how many blacks can there be out here?" Renee chuckled. "Not many, but we're pulling up to my house now, so I'll tell you all about it some other time." Then Renee had a serious look on her face and Hank could sense there was something wrong. It was that same feeling he felt the night of that storm when he saw, "Damm it," he said loudly. "What?" Renee asked. "Here, let me pull into the garage and get you inside; there was an attack on the girls out here." He pulled into the garage and helped Renee get the gear she needed to get everyone started on the antibiotics. The two got out of the van and went into the house.

Ronda was in the kitchen making some tacos. The kids liked that kind of junk food. Miko was in the family room on the phone. She had been trying to reach Mike but hadn't got through to him. She was starting to wonder why he didn't return her pages. All the kids were in the basement playing video games except for Shannon, she wasn't feeling well and was upstairs asleep. When Ronda turned and saw Hank, at first she was relieved, then she focused her eyes on this light-skinned pretty woman and her first thought was, what the fuck is going on? But, before she could even get a word out of her mouth, Miko was right behind her and said, “Hey Hank, who is this?”

Miko’s tone and look indicated she was ready to do both Hank and Renee great bodily harm. You could see the look of disgust on Ronda’s face. Then Renee spoke, “My name is Renee Ward. I’m from the CDC in Atlanta...” Ronda cut her off and said, “Hank what’s going on?” “Hold on ladies, let’s step into the family room and I’ll explain what’s happening here.” “Ok,” Ronda replied, “but first let me feed the kids.” Hank gave the proper introductions and the four adults sat down in the family room. Hank started from the beginning all the way back to the storm including the squirrel carving he and Terrez had seen. Then Miko told about her discovery at the hospital. “Well, Hank, Mrs. Peterson, Miko, there’s an epidemic just waiting to be let loose in this town if not already and I’m going to need all the help I can get to try and stop it.” “What can we do to help?” Miko asked. “Right now let’s get everyone started on these antibiotics. You will have to keep a very close eye on your daughter. Miko keep her isolated from the other children. May I use your phone Hank?” “Of course, it’s right over here.” Hank took her into the living room where the phone was and left her to make her call. Then he asked Ronda if the Sheriff had called. It had been a couple of hours since he'd heard from him last. She told him he hadn't called the house. Renee stepped back into the room with a worried look on her face and told the three, she was unable to reach Sam and Dave. "Well, is it possible they left?" Hank said. "Yes, but they know to check in." "Well, maybe they finished and went to the hotel," Hank replied. "Yes, it's possible, could you take me there? I need to speak with them. I also have to call my boss back in Atlanta. We need to get in touch with the Sheriff and Jacob. Miko you should be able to administer the shots being a nurse's assistant." Renee was being very direct she knew they didn't have much time. Then she turned to Hank and said, "Ready? We have to move quickly." "Yes," Hank said. Then he turned to Ronda and said, "Keep the kids inside, I'll be back shortly." Ronda said, "Excuse me Mrs. Ward. Hank can I talk to you for a second privately?" "It's Miss, Mrs. Peterson," Renee replied.

Ronda took Hank into the living room. "Why do you have to go? Why can't you stay here with us?" Ronda asked. "Ronda," Hank said, "if I don't go, who is? I mean, how many people do you think know about what's happening here? It's not as if it's in the Newton Times." He grabbed her, kissed her and told her he loved her. Hank and Renee Ward left.

Miko went into the living room with her sister and said, "I don't like that bitch and you better watch her. She wants your husband." "Yeah, I know," Ronda answered. "But she did come over here and try to save us from the Plague."

Chapter 20

The Sheriff had left the deli. The two doctors ordered a couple of turkey sandwiches and another round of drinks. Lou Spellman was extremely nervous and confused now. All he had set out to do was find out if the allegations about Dr. Josh Jackson and Professor Lisa Straub being his parents were true. He had also become intrigued about the sixth floor—for he knew the answers to some of his questions lie between the key, the flashing lights and the sixth floor.

Dr. Going began to speak. "Lou," he called him instead of doctor for the first time. "Years ago, I had a colleague named Josh Jackson. This is the friend of mines whose house you now reside in. He like you was from Michigan. He met and fell in love with and married a beautiful woman from Michigan also. Her name was Lisa Straub. She was a professor at one of the best Scientific Universities in the country—Wayne State Medical Center. The two of them like all scientists had a dream of curing all diseases known to mankind. They moved to Asia and for years they worked on cloning, genetic engineering, regeneration, and hybridization. They had a child and sent the child back to the States because the Plague was spreading rapidly through Asia." Lou knew what was coming next. Dr. Going took another drink and said, "Lou Spellman, you are that child. When I heard you had moved to Iowa and went to Bedford Hospital, I knew it wouldn't be long before Chapman got to you. And he did get to you, didn't he?" "Yes," Spellman answered. "Then why did you lie to the Sheriff and tell him you didn't know him?" "I just got nervous. With all that's been happening and then, he said Chapman was dead. I didn't know what to say." "Well, we'll deal with him later, "Going said," But for now I need you to listen very carefully. Your mother and father were on the verge of a major scientific breakthrough when she got ill and I brought them back to the States. Once they were back, the three of us worked feverishly on their new theory. We took to the notion that if we took physical Mutagens along with the cloning and hybridization process that we would be able to produce new clean disease free body organs. This in fact would wipe out all diseases known to mankind. There would be no more waiting on donor organs; we could just manufacture them and the world would have to pay trillions for this knowledge. In fact, we tried it and the process worked." "You tried it on humans?" Dr. Spellman asked in disbelief. "Of course not, we tried it on the squirrels." "The squirrels," replied Spellman. "Yes, the squirrels," Going said.

Going waved to the young waitress for the check. "We need to get back to the hospital and I need to get into your basement. There are still a few loose ends that have to be tied up before we're ready to go public." The waitress came with the check, Going paid the bill and the two doctors left. Lou Spellman had a lot of questions that he needed answered but for now he just needed to think. To clear his head, he told Going that he was going to go home and asked him to get someone to fill in for him. "Of course, I understand the shock this must be to you but you are to say nothing of this to anyone. I'll stop by your house later tonight. Get some rest and clear your head; we still have a lot of work to do".

They were at the hospital now and Spellman remembered he still had to deal with Mike. Going still hadn't heard from fat Lou. He knew he had to call his sister back and tell her something. Lou Spellman walked to his car and decided he would deal with Mike later. Right now he needed to be alone.

Chapter 21

Hank and Renee arrived at the Newton Holiday Inn. Ms. Renee Ward went to check in and see if Dave and Sam had arrived. The clerk told her that neither of the men had called or checked in. Renee found this to be strange—they knew the routine.

Meantime, Hank was trying to get in touch with the Sheriff and had no luck. The Sheriff had been trying to contact Jacob but he also had no luck. His head was pounding now and he was starting to get the chills and sweat all at the same time. The Sheriff stopped at the local drug store and decided to get some more aspirin and called it a night. After the Sheriff coughed, spread his germs all over the store and infected everyone there, he headed home.

When he opened the front door his wife could see he was looking quite pale and sick. His son, Casey was just about to run and give his father a hug when his mother shouted, "No, Casey! No. Your father looks ill, go watch TV. Honey, are you alright?" "Don't know, my head's killing me and my whole body feels sore." "Here let me get you to bed. Do you want me to get you a doctor?" "No," he said, coughing and choking. "Get me those aspirins and call Hank Peterson." His wife put him to bed, gave him the aspirin and wiped him down. She then coughed a couple of times and figured she'd put Casey to bed and lay down herself. She tucked the boy in, infecting him also and laid down on the couch. She would call Hank Peterson in the morning.

Renee had the bellboy take her bags to her room and asked Hank if he would like a drink. "Sure," Hank said. "I could use two right about now." The two of them got a small booth in the corner and ordered some drinks and a light snack. "I'm really worried about Sam, Dave and Jacob. Where could they be?" "I'm sure they're ok; sometimes Jacob is known for hanging at the gentlemen's club here in town, so he probably took Sam and Dave with him to check out the ladies." "I suppose, but they know better than to not check in with me." "What are you their mother or something?" Hank said. And no sooner than he finished the statement, he knew he had said the wrong thing. Renee glared at him and said, "Excuse me you know on second thought I think I'll just take the bottle of wine to my room." "Please bring the van over first thing in the morning," she said and got up, stopped at the bar, got a bottle of wine and stormed out.

The waitress came over and asked if everything was okay and if he still wanted his two margaritas. Hank said "yes" and just sat there. By this time he was getting a little tired. He drank the drinks and kept thinking about the past few days. Then it hit him—that squirrel on Somerset! He would check it out in the morning. Hank finished his drinks and drove home.

Renee Ward was bone tired, she opened her wine, drank a glass and decided to take a long soak; but first she had to call the Director of the CDC. She knew he would be upset nothing had gone according to the book. She should have checked in hours ago. She called him at his home. Bear Russell was a medium built Latino, mixed with Indian, who had studied biology at the University of Arizona. He was a well-known chemist and had come up with many of the cures involving animals and humans. President Clinton had personally picked him, to head up the CDC, which had been known for its lack of diversity of high-ranking employees. Russell had bought in numerous amounts of minorities and demanded perfection from each.

Renee Ward knew she was about to get an earful. "Hello." "Hi Bear," Renee started to say. "Don't hi me," Bear said. "What the hell is going on and why haven't you checked in?" "Sir…" "Quiet, let me finish, I've had the goddamn Mayor of Newton busting my balls all day. He says you want to seal off the town. He says there have been no reports of the Plague and that you're about to start up a panic just in time for their fair. Now what the shit is going on there? And why did it take you seven hours to check in?" Renee explained how Sam and Dave were missing and about the events of the past two days as she understood them. "Then, why has the hospital not contacted us?" Russell demanded to know. "I'm not sure sir but I think it has something to do with our friend, Dr. Lou Spellman." "Spellman," the Director blurted. "Don't tell me that arrogant son of a bitch is there and has something to do with this?" "I'm afraid so, sir but I need a little more time to prove it. In the meantime I need to get a warning out to the general public. If this thing starts spreading, we could lose this whole town. I have to have a little muscle to move around. Send me more vaccines and a couple more men sir." "Ward, how much time do we have?" "Sir, thirty-six to forty-eight hours at the most. I need twelve to prove it." "Ward, you have eight hours starting at seven in the morning. After that, you know I have to contact our friend, Jenkins, the Army and the National Guard." "But sir…" "No buts, Ward, do your fucking job and get me something to go on! Find me a cure, some type of containment…and Ward, get some sleep. You sound like shit and I'm sure you look worst. Goodnight." Bear Russell slammed down the phone and went to pour himself a drink.

Renee Ward took a hot soak, drank her wine and decided that she would call in a couple of favors first thing in the morning. She needed her own team on this and she knew just the team she would need to get into town without causing too much suspicion. The guys at the CDC were good but it always took too much red tape to get things done. She couldn't risk the careers of these guys at CDC because they had families. Yes, she said to herself. She would make the call.

Chapter 22

It was dark and his head was pounding like a bad hangover. The floor was cold and he couldn't move. He tried to remember where he was and what had happened to him. Mike had been out cold for more than ten hours. Suddenly in the distant coming from afar, down the hall he hear it, the sound of gnawing. Then he remembered he was on the sixth floor. He had come to look for fat Lou and to find out what was going on up there. What was that Going's trying to hide? Only now he wished he had listened to Going and stayed away. Why would someone club him and tie him up he wondered? And worst than that who and what were they going to do with him? Now he was helpless, could not do anything but wait and see what lie ahead.

Chapter 23

It was about 11:00 o'clock and the town seemed quiet except for a few clubs. The morning would be different there was sure to be lots going on. The motels would be full of vendors checking in for the fair. Dammit, Hank thought to himself, if there was a plague going around this could be disastrous. They would have to move fast in the morning to put all the pieces together. He got out of the van and was startled by the sound in the trees. He hurried and got into the house. After looking around, everyone was asleep so he just sat on the couch staring at the TV, until he nodded off. In other parts of town everything was not as quiet as it seemed, plans were being made. When Dr. Going, returned to the hospital he was informed that his sister Katie had been calling every ten minutes or so. That meant that fat Lou still hadn't made it home. He called her, tried to calm her down but she was hysterical and sobbing uncontrollably. He instructed her to take a xanax and that he would see her first thing in the morning. Then they would contact the sheriff. She did so and passed out for the night. Going then called the head nurse and had her find out the status of TJ. There had been a change in his condition he was really getting worst. Going decided to let him try to fight it off until morning instead of increasing his dosage. He then had Mike paged. He was supposed to be working that night and Going had not heard from him since earlier. He waited about five minutes and had him paged again, still nothing. He knew something strange was going on. He wondered had Mike gone to the sixth floor against his orders and what about fat Lou? He had to get over to Spellman's house that's where all this would unfold. He also had to be careful he had laid a lot of information on Spellman and didn't want him to panic. He was too close now and could smell the money. Going called Spellman, "Hello." "Hello Doctor this is Going, hope you got a little rest. I checked on the kid and he's stable but I do have a few concerns about a couple of other matters." "Like what sir?" Spellman replied. "Not on the phone I'm coming over there tonight. I'll tell you then, see you in about thirty minutes." "That's fine," Spellman answered and hung up. Meanwhile Mike heard the pages, was struggling to get lose but he was in the dark and could not find anything to work with to set himself loose.

Chapter 24

Renee Ward slipped into the tub, was thinking about Hank and how she felt close to him. She was sorry she reacted the way she had. She imagined he was there in the room with her. He stepped into the bathroom with her, took a soap sponge and began to wash her back. She asked him, "Do you really think we can beat this thing?" "I don't know but we sure as hell aren't going to take it lying down." She stood up, revealed her lustrous round 36 double "D" breasts, beautiful athletic toned body to him and motioned for a towel. He wrapped the Matrix bath sheet around her and took her into his arms. First, he kissed her on her forehead then her neck. She grabbed him, kissed him and slowly began undressing him. Hank picked her up and carried her to the bedroom. As they fell back on to the bed she remember he was a married man but she also knew her body ached for attention. Hank knew he was wrong but put it out of his head. Here was this beautiful woman whom he would probably never see or hear from again. He walked away and returned with a tube of hot oil. Renee lay there naked on her stomach and showed signs of tenseness as he began to pour the oil down her back and unto her buttocks. As he started to massage the oil onto her shoulders and back, she could feel the power from his grip and longed for him to take control of her body filling her burning desires. Hank felt a need to hold this beautiful woman in his arms, to feel the warmth of her vagina circling his penis. He lowered his hand and caressed her lower back with smooth gentle even strokes. He turned her over and poured oil onto her awaiting breast down to her navel and slowly down each leg. She could see his manhood was at full attention and wasn't sure how much longer she could hold on. This time he started massaging from below and worked his way up. He caressed her thighs, climbed on top of her and thrust his penis into her warm moist vagina.

He penetrated her with slow, smooth strokes. She climbed on top and rode him like a bull-rider in a Texas rodeo. They shift to the doggie style position and both came like a winter blizzard in Michigan. The room was hot she opened the windows to get some air. Hank put on his clothes, kissed her told he would see her in the morning and left. Renee just laid there amongst their scents of love making and let the breeze blow where it may.

She thought she heard something, a noise coming from the other room. It was getting louder she went to take a peak and something flew by her head. She saw what appeared to be a flying squirrel and started to scream. Her scream was cut short by a squirrel that flew into her mouth and bit her tongue. Then hundreds of squirrels flew into the room and started attacking her. She slipped under the water and dropped the wineglass. She came up choking and shaking. It had been a dream, a nightmarish dream and she was scared. Around that same time, Hank woke up in front of the TV. He went upstairs and climbed into bed with his wife. Renee got out of the tub, dried off, checked the window and went to bed.

Chapter 25

Just about that time, Dr. Going arrived at Lou Spellman's house. He pulled into the driveway and went to the front door. Spellman saw him pull up so he was at the door to let him in. "Come in sir, please come on in." Spellman, rested had come to grips with what Going's told him earlier and wanted nothing more than to finish his mother and father's work. After all, he had idolized the man for years and wanted to know everything about him. Dr. Going brought his notes with him. He'd kept them hidden at the hospital, locked in a safe no one knew about. The two men went to the basement.

"Yes, it looks just the way it did years ago," Going said. "Let me ask you son did you happen to find a key?" "Well yes, but how did you know about that?" "Well if you know your history it kind of sums it all up. The key was the reason your father and I chose this place. Have you used it yet?" "Yes, but then these weird lights would start blinking and I didn't have the guts to follow them to the end." "That was very smart of you Doctor, you see back in the early nineteen hundreds this town was a military base. A very proud and eccentric general by the name of Hawkins was in charge. The hospital was the command quarters and the general lived in this house. He had a tunnel built leading from this house to the hospital. In fact right to the labs on the sixth floor. Nobody knew about the labs. When the base closed down it was gutted and turned into a hospital. Nobody knew about the tunnel until your father happened to discover the door and we found the original blueprints that were kept secret for national security reasons. We need to go thru the tunnel and get into the labs. That's where we kept the squirrels." "But aren't we in danger of being attacked?" "Of course we are but if memory serves me right about a quarter mile before we get to the labs there should be some suits and some poison repellant. We can use these to keep them off us just long enough to get to the final notes we need. People at the hospital are starting to hear noises and it won't be long before we're found out. So grab the key and let's go. Also get a couple of flashlights while you're at it."

Chapter 26

"There's one more thing I failed to mention Spellman and that is my sisters husband Lou from Klean & Klean has been missing for about twenty hours now. I fear he may have run into trouble up in one of the labs." "I knew it I caught one of the janitors sneaking around up there earlier today." "Well where is he now?" "I fear it's the young man I sent to search for Lou." "Well I kind of knocked him out and drugged him. He's still up there bounded and gagged." "Good we will have to dispose of him before he can tell anyone." "Well there's one more thing. Yesterday when they brought in the little boy, while I was speaking to his mother and the sheriff." He paused, "spit it out man it's too late to turn back now!" "Well two women came busting out of the stairway that leads to the sixth floor. I did some checking and one of them works there. I also found out she's been asking a lot of questions about the sixth floor." The two men were at the spot where they needed to get the suits and poison repellant. The lights were blinking as always when the door was opened.

Spellman put on the suit, as did Going. They sprayed each other down with the toxin and continued to the lab. "Are you sure this will keep them off us? I wouldn't want to end up like Doctor Chapman, I heard he was mutilated and eaten down to the bones." "I'm sure after all I had a hand in creating them." "Why are they so vicious," Spellman asked? "Because we had to use some human brain DNA and the only place to get it was from a death row inmate who had killed, murdered and mutilated three families." "So with the right DNA we can do the regeneration process without the violent side effects. We're home free to crossbreed human organs from healthy people and make a fortune."

The men were at the back door to lab 621 now and could hear the gnawing. "How do we get in?" "The key it fits both doors." "There's one more thing I have to know. They say my parent's disappeared. I need to know what really happen?" "Son, are you sure you want to know, are you really sure?" "Yes I am…we've come this far and swept this many skeletons out the closet, why not a few more?" "That's just it, that's exactly what we may find in here."

Chapter 27

(Flashback)

It was nineteen ninety-one, Josh Jackson and his wife Lisa had just landed back in the states after almost twenty years of being gone. Lisa was pretty ill from the effects of the plague and not being able to contact her son, Lou Spellman. He was given that name by chance in case someone tried to follow his or her research. Dr. Going, Josh's good friend and colleague picked them up from the airport. He arranged for Josh to purchase the house on Somerset. He and Josh had brought Lisa back to decent health. That's when they discovered that human and animal DNA could be mixed under the right circumstances causing new organs to be generically produced. They all agreed that they would have to try it on Lisa or she would die.

By now they had genetically engineered hundreds of crossbred squirrels and were mixing them with aborted fetuses and Stem cells. The only problem was the baby stem cells had no clear pattern of thought so they needed a stem cell from an adult. This research still being illegal in the states created a problem. That's when they came up with the answer, an adult stem cell. But where would they get it? Going's was the one to come up with the ideal of getting it from someone admitted to the hospital that didn't have a chance to live. They took a gun shot victim, removed DNA and stole the brain. This is where they got their stem cells from not knowing he was a fugitive wanted for murder.

After the transfusions Lisa started having strange side effects, violent episodes. There was no choice but to take her back up to the lab and check the records, which were left from the testing. Upon returning to lab 621, she became uncontrollably violent and started to unlock the squirrel cages knocking them over and releasing the deadly squirrels. Josh tried to help her but I remember panicking and running out the door. I still hear their screams at night as I heard the squirrels ripping them apart.

(*Present*)

"Are you ready Lou?" Spellman stood still for a moment then gathered himself, "yes I'm ready." The gnawing loud and mind boggling brought fears that were of the hellish imagination. But, still the thought of all world riches consumed the two doctors to press on. The key worked…they had opened the back door to lab 621.

Chapter 28

It was now around 3:00 am, the playboy mayor/judge was just finishing getting his rocks off. He dismissed the cute young townswomen like a prisoner freed on personal bail. She went to her car and drove off. On her way home she made the biggest mistake of her young life. She was thirsty again, this time not for dick cream but for pop. She stopped in the 24-hour shop and convinced herself that route 99 would be a quicker way to get home. The mayor meanwhile drove himself home drank a beer and went to sleep. The fair was only a day and a half away. As the young cutie was driving down the old highway, she noticed her gas was low. She cursed herself for not getting any at the 24-hour shop. Then her car started to stall.

Sara, that was her name, got out the car cursing herself and tried to call her former lover she never knew what hit her. The last thing she saw was a tiny figure, leap toward her. She felt deaf defying pain from the flesh ripping squirrels. The squirrels feasted on her for about twenty minutes until nothing but her skeleton was left.

Morning was approaching and the two doctors knew they had to hurry. As they stepped into the lab the first thing they saw was hundreds of squirrels, some flying over their heads, others running around them looking confused but not daring to attack. This meant the poison toxin was working. Doctor Going told Spellman to search the files toward the front of the lab and look for the file labeled Genetic Mutation. Doctor Spellman was just about to go toward the front, when he saw two skeletons lying on the floor very close together, as if one was trying to cover the other. He could only imagine what had happen and he knew it had to be his parents lying there in that pile of dried up blood and bones. He started to vomit and was about to remove his headgear when Going stopped him. "No! Leave it on or they will kill you." He swallowed his own vomit. "We don't have much time the effects of the poison only last twenty to thirty minutes. Let's start searching man now!"

Spellman went to the front and that's when he saw what used to be a very large man's remains in fresh blood. "Going over here. Did you find it? No, but I think I've found your sisters husband." "Fuck him! Look for the file man and hurry!" Going himself was frantically looking threw drawers and files but saw nothing. "It has to be here!" Then he saw it a bright red folder labeled Genetic Mutation. "I have it let's go!" The squirrels were making a terrible racket that could be heard on the floors below but no one dared to come up on six to see what it was. Mike heard it to and was shaking terribly he had wet his pants.

Just as the two men were about to leave, Going stopped and asked, "Where's Mike?" "What?" "Mike where is he?" "Down the hall but you can't be thinking." "Look we have all we need but there can't be any witnesses or trails leading to us. We'll feed him to the squirrels and later figure out how to kill them, clean up these remains and we'll be home free. Now where is he we only have five minutes left?" The two men stepped over fat Lou's remains. "Try not to let any of them out." The two men squeezed out the door being careful not to let any of the creatures out, or lock the door. They hurried down the hall to where Mike was. As they carried him, Mike struggled for his life sweating like in a sauna. Then his bowels went loose. "Should we knock him out first?" "No time, we only have two minutes left." They opened the door to the lab the squirrels could smell Mike and they attacked him immediately. Mike fully conscious was totally helpless as the squirrels feasted on him. His last thought was what had he done to deserve this kind of death?

Spellman and Going exited the way they came. As soon as they sealed the door back Spellman ripped his suit off and started throwing up. He had seen a lot as a doctor but never a human being eaten alive and it made him sick to his stomach. Going had this big smile as if he'd just won the lottery. In a sense he had.

Chapter 29

Back at Spellman's house Going instructed Spellman to burn the suits while he looked over the files. Spellman did so in a daze, he couldn't get the picture of his parent's bones lying in that pile of dried up blood or Mike being eaten alive out his head. Yet he still did as Going's ordered. He now was a doctor and murderer. There was no turning back. He knew he had to watch his back. Going was cold, heartless and he knew now that they had the missing files Going would let nothing or no one stop him. This discovery could really make a difference and save more lives than he ever dreamed of. Not to mention his parents were the rightful owners of the experiments. He decided he would go along. In science, after all, everyone knows there has to be a few sacrifices for the good of many. This discovery was going to make him one of the richest men in the world.

"Spellman, this appears to be it but we don't have time right now. It's four-thirty and I need you at the hospital by eight. In the meantime, I have to take my sister to file a missing persons report with the sheriff in the morning. Take a hot shower clear your head and I'll see you at the hospital later. I'll just hold on to this file for safekeeping." Spellman didn't like it but didn't want to show any signs of mistrust. "Alright," Spellman replied, as the two men headed upstairs to the door, "see you then." Dr. Going drove home gloating and smiling like the joker in a Batman movie. Spellman, did exactly what Going said took a very long hot shower.

Chapter 30

It was 5:45 am and Renee was up. She decided to have coffee and a donut before making her call. She wanted to clear her head of the nightmare the night before. Bear Russell had given her just eight hours to get the proof she needed to seal off the town and the clock would start ticking at seven. Renee finished her coffee, grabbed her phone book from her purse and looked up Volen Hughes, the billionaire. She'd met Mr. Hughes while she was a student at the University of Washington. Hughes had donated a lot of money to the research program there and Renee had met him once when he was being honored. He knew about her talents in biotechnology and had called on her for a favor once she'd become the Assistant Director of the (EPO) office at the (CDC). He told her about how he'd funded the tests in Asia. He also knew about the child that Josh and Lisa had sent back to the states. Hughes had slowed down the funding he was sending Lisa because of the lack of results. He also didn't care much for Josh. He felt Josh was drawing Lisa away from the research she should have truly been doing. He'd found out that Josh, had been stealing monies and along with his friend Dr. Going, had started a corporation called Clone-Be-Right or (C.B.R.). Renee dialed the number.

Hughes was just finishing his morning swim. He was up by four o'clock everyday so this was the time to catch him without going threw his staff. "Hello." "Good morning Mr. Hughes. I'm sorry to bother you this early in the morning but I'm in desperate need of your help." "Alright but don't you think you should tell me who this is first? This is a private number so I imagine we've met at one point or another." "Forgive me sir." She said to herself, how could I be so stupid asking this man for help and not even said who I am. But there was no time for second guessing, time was moving fast and she knew Newton didn't have a lot of it left. "This is Renee Ward from the (CDC), we've met a few times." "Yes, I know who you are. How are you doing? It's been way to long. Are you in town?" "No, sir but I need you to listen to me very carefully." "Then by all means Ms. Ward, speak up you have my full attention." "Thank you, sir."

She talked to Hughes for about a half-hour, explaining everything that had happen in Newton and how she guessed Spellman was involved. There was silence for about five seconds. "Alright, tell you what I'm going to do. I'll give you my best man Alex Reed; you do remember Alex don't you?" "Yes, sir and thank you." "Hold on not so fast, you have to do something for me too." She listened very carefully and then agreed. "Good then we have a deal. Alex will call you within the next ten minutes. You have him at your disposal for forty-eight hours and at the end of that time, I should have what I need and you should have accomplished your mission." "Thank you sir," Renee said and hung up the phone. Her next call was to the front desk to see if Sam and Dave had ever checked in although she feared the worst.

She told Bear to send more men. They should have arrived late last night and met her in the lobby at seven o'clock this morning. Renee hurried and got dressed. She slipped on a pair of jeans that fit perfectly and a white short sleeve shirt that showed just enough cleavage to stir the imagination. She put her gun in her purse along with some vales of a drug and about ten needles. "Shit!" Renee walked over to her suitcase, picked up a couple of clips, about two boxes of bullets and shoved them in her purse. By most standards it was considered really big. One might call it a little briefcase. The phone rang it was Alex Reed, Volen Hughes personal bodyguard.

Alex Reed was an ex-Navy-Seal who served in the Gulf War, the CIA and was not the type of man you wanted to challenge. He worked for Hughes for the last fifteen years. Alex was just who Renee was hoping to get. She knew him in fact they were intimate for a short time when she worked at the CDC in Spokane, Washington. "Good morning Renee how have you been? I've been meaning to call you." "Cut the bull Alex, how long before you can get here?" "Ninety minutes give or take a few. Did Mr. Hughes fill you in?" "Yes he did but if I know you there's more right?" "Yes, there is so listen up." She told Alex the story with a few more details. "Okay, Renee I'm going to bring two men with me we'll need their help." "That's fine just hurry." "You got it, call you soon as we get airborne." Volen Hughes had already called ahead and had a chopper waiting. Alex called two of his most dependable men who served under him on some of his most dangerous missions. Renee took her briefcase and headed for the lobby. Before Alex left, Volen called him to the table where he was looking over the stock market. "This is it Alex, I can feel it be sure to get the package." "Yes Sir, Mr. Hughes," Alex said as he started for the chopper. "Alex there's one more thing you should know. I made a few calls and if they have to shut down the town they will bring in your friend Jenkins." "I understand Sir, see you in forty-eight hours."

At seven o'clock, Hank and Ronda were up and in the kitchen. Hank munching on some leftovers; he was already dressed and ready to go. Ronda hadn't said anything yet she was fixing breakfast. She turned to Hank with this dazed kind of glare and said. "Hank do you love me?" "Of course baby," moving toward her. He grabbed her butt "and why do you ask?" He was about to kiss her when Terrez came around the corner, "what are you doing dad?" "Hey Terrez," they were both surprised. Hank released her butt, "nothing son just talking to your mother."

Terrez asked what was for breakfast and went into the family room to watch cartoons. "Pancakes," Ronda answered. Hank had just grabbed his keys when it came. He knew that was going to be the next question of the morning. "Where are you going," Ronda asked, with that look on her face? "Honey this thing still isn't over. I still have Renee's van." "Oh," she jumped in now "you two are on a first name basis." "Ronda please…don't, start. What I need you to do is make sure Miko gives everyone their shot and keep the kids in the house and the phone line open." He went to give her a kiss and she turned her head away from him. He shouted to Terrez on the way out the door. "See you later man be careful." "Bye daddy, see you," Terrez said. Hank got into the van started it and drove off. He picked up his cell phone and called Renee. "Good morning about last night, I." Renee stopped him, "Hank there's no need we were both tired. How far are you?" "I'm about ten minutes away." "Well hurry we don't have any time to spare." As soon as he hung up his phone rang. He knew it was Ronda but he was wrong. It was Sheriff Brown's wife.

She told Hank about how Sheriff Brown looked last night and now he was worst. “I’m scared, Mr. Peterson, please come help us,” she said with a cough. “Give me forty minutes, Mrs. Brown, I’m on my way.” Hank called his mother next, “Hello.” “Morning mom, how are you?” “I’m okay, just a little sad about Red-Dog.” “Yeah I know fucking shame. But, the reason I called is I want you to pack up some stuff and get out of town.” “What,” she said, “why?” “I can’t answer all your questions now. You have to get out of this town ASAP.” “Hank,” she started to say and he cut her off. She hadn’t ever heard this tone in her son’s voice. She got the gut feeling that a mother gets when something’s about to happen to one of her children. “Mom just trust me and do it. I’ll try to explain later but just get packed and ready to get the hell out of Newton.” Hank hung up the phone and pulled into the lobby entrance of the hotel. He still needed answers, some substance to go along with his own suspicions. Hank had that feeling again that there was something terribly wrong in Newton. He had to get his family out.

Chapter 31

It was about seven fifteen when Going's arrived at his sisters. He had showered, shaved and was on his second cup of coffee with only a couple hours of sleep. He was use to the routine in fact most doctors rarely got enough sleep. Going pulled his red corvette in front of his sister's house. He called and let her know he was on the way, so when he pulled up she came right out. She looked as if she hadn't slept at all but had been doing a lot of crying. Going got out the car and gave her a big hug. "Come on Katie everything's going to be fine we'll find him." Going kept a straight face as he told her that lie. He knew fat Lou was dead. He also knew how he had died. In fact, he had planned it that way. They pulled off and headed for the sheriff's office.

Dr. Spellman was on his way to the hospital. He figured he would check on TJ before meeting with Going later. When he got to the hospital it was in sort of an uproar. “What’s happening here?” Spellman asked the nurse at the front desk, who had a mask over her face and gloves on her hands. “I’m not sure Doctor but we sure could use your help.” “Tell me what you do know then.” “Okay but follow me. Well last night the head nurse on duty started complaining about a headache and she started vomiting. We took her to one of the rooms on the second floor and let her lie down. I took her temperature and she was running a slight fever. We called for a doctor but everyone was busy. When we went back to check on her she was in this condition.” Spellman opened the door to the room where the nurse was. He saw what was once a beautiful young nurse, looking like she had been beaten in the face with a baseball bat. Her face was a deep purple color, eyes were bloodshot and she was vomiting. Spellman closed the door. “Isolate this room, no this floor, has anyone else checked in with headaches, vomiting or anything? Get me a list of anyone who came in contact with her and get it now!”

Spellman was horrified at what he saw. He ran to TJ's room and TJ's mother was outside crying. She looked up at Spellman and screamed. "You bastard! You fucking bastard!" She jumped up at Spellman and the guard had to pull her off him. "Where were you…where were you?" Spellman entered the room. TJ had the same discoloration that he'd just seen in the nurse. He knew for certain that the "PLAGUE" or "BLACK DEATH" as some called it was upon the town of Newton, Iowa.

Chapter 32

As Hank walked into the hotel lobby, he saw Renee talking with two men. He walked up to her and asked if everything was all right. "I'm not sure Sam and Dave never showed up, this is Thomas and Alfred." Hank reached out and shook the two men's hands. She introduced Hank as one of the locals who was helping out. Renee told the two men to have a seat while she spoke to Hank alone. Renee explained about the call she'd made, how she didn't want to risk the careers of the two men by having them break the rules or the law for that matter. She also sensed something very bad was happening.

Hank told her about the call he'd gotten from the sheriff's wife and they both agreed they had better get over their, ASAP. Renee told Thomas and Alfred to follow them in the car they had rented last night. She followed Hank to the van climbed in and asked Hank if he'd taken his shot. "No." "Well then it's time," she said and pulled out her needle. Hank drove to the sheriff's house. On the way he tried to call Jacob but there was no answer. Renee instructed Thomas and Alfred to wait behind in the car and to keep trying Dave and Sam on the phone. Hank and Renee went up to the door and rang the bell. The sheriff's wife looking very pale came to the door.

"Are you all right," Hank asked? "Yes, it's Tyrone he's in there." As soon as she opened the door and Renee saw the sheriff she quickly closed it. "What are you doing?" "Just bear with me for a minute," Renee answered and went to the van. She grabbed a mask, some gloves and her needles. "You two better wait out here," she said. Renee went into the room she had seen these symptoms before. Tyrone Brown had the plague and who knew how many people he'd come in contact with. She gave him a shot, then his wife and son. She had Hank call for an ambulance to take all of them to the hospital. The sheriff needed to tell Hank something before they left. Renee told Hank he shouldn't come in contact with the sheriff. She gave the sheriff a pen and paper to write down his message. Renee took the note, told his wife help was on the way and they left. Hank told her he would see her at the hospital. It was time to find out what exactly had happen to Jacob, Dave and Sam.

"What just happened back there?" Hank asked this as they pulled away from the house. "It's the plague, the sheriff and his family are infected with the plague. God, this is what I was afraid of. We have to get this town sealed off and start getting these people some vaccines. Now lets get to the clinic and see what's going on with Jacob, Sam and Dave." In the meantime, Dr. Going and his sister had just pulled up to the sheriff's office. They entered and stumbled upon a pale looking deputy.

"Is Sheriff Brown here," Going's asked? "No he took ill and had to be taken to the hospital," the deputy answered. "Well we would like to file a missing person's report." The deputy took all the information and assured Katie they would find her husband. Dr. Going drove his sister back home and told her he would follow up on the deputies' promise and not to worry. "Here take a couple of these," he said and gave her some sleeping pills. "I'll call you later but right now I have to get to work." He walked his sister to the door gave her a kiss and left.

Going called Spellman from his car to find out what was going on. Spellman told him about the nurse and TJ. "Dr. Going, we have to call the CDC. We now have confirmed cases of the plague." "No, are you crazy? We're too close. Keep your mouth shut and wait till I get there. I have to stop by the mayor's office." "But, what about this plague," Spellman asked? "Take your shots, don't worry about the others, isolate them and tell them it's an amthax outbreak and that the vaccine is due tomorrow." "There's one more thing Dr. Going, they just brought the sheriff in and he's been infected. What do you suppose we do about that?" "Great! Let the old bastard die."

Chapter 33

Ronda had finished cooking breakfast. Miko and the rest of the kids were up. "What's happening," Miko asked? "I'm not sure," Ronda said. "Hank took off to go meet that bitch. He said to be sure to give everyone his or her shot." "Fine," Miko said, "but there's some strange shit going on. I still haven't talked to Mike. Maybe I should go to the hospital." "No, Miko I need you here with the kids and I." The phone rang, "hello," Ronda answered. "Hi Ronda it's JP, where's Hank and what's going on? He told me to get out of Newton today." Terrez, Jasmine, Tash and Porter had all been listening, Shannon too, she was up and feeling better.

Ronda told JP about the attack on the kids and the hand that they had found. "If I heard you right Ronda, what you're saying is that the town is infested with killer squirrels?" "I don't know for sure but those are the facts, as I know them." "Then call your husband and get my grandchildren out of here!"

Chapter 34

Hank, Renee, Thomas and Alfred pulled up to the clinic. The atmosphere presented an eerie feeling with its quietness. In fact, it was to quiet. Hank was about to approach the door when Renee called him back to the van. "Wait put this on." The four of them suited up with the protective gear and walked toward the door. Hank tried to open the door and gave it a hard push. He looked inside, his jaws released a salty liquid and he started to gag. His stomach was about to erupt with vomit, his eyes got glazy and his knees felt weak. He backed up and closed the door. "GOD NO!" "What is it?" "Don't go in there." "Alfred, take care of Mr. Peterson. Thomas you ready," she screamed. "Ready." They stepped in the room and blood was everywhere.

Their entrance had just crumbled the remains of Sam. Renee was trying to be strong. She stepped over Sam's mutilated bones and Thomas followed. In the next room they went stepping over and in what seemed to be piles and piles of blood, cloth and human skeletons that had been eaten alive. She instructed Thomas to get a few samples of everything and went back outside. Hank was at the back of the van in a state of shock. He had never seen or wanted to see the total mutilation of the human skeleton system, twice. Renee walked up to him, "we have a serious problem. Get me to the mayor's office." Her phone rang it was Alex Reed. He was in Newton, Iowa. Dr. Going arrived at the mayor/judges office and went directly in to see him.

"Mr. Mayor, how are you?" Going asked as he shook the mayor's hand. "Just fine Doc and you?" "I couldn't be better. We do have a bit of a problem though sit down let me pour you a drink." "Brandy, ok?" "Sure that will be fine but make it a double. Last night Dr. Spellman and I found the missing notes for the cloning/regeneration experiments." "That's great news," the mayor said as he took a seat himself. "I think that deserves a toast." "It in itself does," Going replied, as he raised his glass to the mayor's. "Well now man what is this problem." "It's the plague, Newton is about to become infected with it." "Dammit! Then that bitch was right." "What bitch?" "Some whore from the CDC is in town." "What who called her? I never authorized anything like that. It didn't come from my staff." "Yes, I know I believe it was our dear sheriff and the local vet." The mayor told Going about his visit from Sheriff Brown. "I've already contacted the director of the CDC in Atlanta. So, we still have time to fix or deny this whole plague thing." "But, what about the squirrels," the Mayor asked? "Can you contain them? According to the sheriff there have been at least two attacks and one death. You know tomorrow is the fair at least five million in revenue is at stake." "Mr. Mayor, did you hear what I said? Screw the fair and the people of this little shit-hole town! We're talking worldwide profits this is going to make us the richest most powerful men on the planet. Listen very close, do exactly as I tell you and we'll come out of this thing just fine. As far as the people of Newton, we'll let the government and the CDC deal with them. First, we deny any reports of killer squirrels or any reported cases of the plague. I'll handle the hospital you handle the media just in case the word has gotten out. If no one asks about it then you don't tell! Let the fair go on no matter what." This is what the mayor wanted to hear all along.

Going outlined his plan step by step to the mayor. He wasn't worried about him not doing what he asked because the mayor/judge of Newton owned twenty percent of the shares of Clones-Be-Right. Going's himself, owned thirty percent and the other fifty-percent belonged to investors all around the world including, Volen Hughes. In fact, the shares of CBR had fallen to their lowest. This was just right for a take over but no one would risk it. As far as the other investor knew, the research was a disaster and everyone was selling the shares. All but one investor, he was buying but no one knew yet. The mayor's phone rang he picked it up and told his secretary that he was in a meeting. Whoever it was would have to wait. Going finished his drink, got up, that's when the door busted open with Hank and Renee storming in. The mayor's secretary ran in behind them. "Sorry sir, I couldn't stop them." "I see you're about to be busy," Going said. "I'll contact you later," he said and left.

Hank nor Renee knew Going's so they didn't recognize him. "What's the meaning of this and who the hell are you? Call security then call the sheriff!" "Sir, sorry to bust in on you but this can't wait. My name is Renee Ward, I'm from the CDC." "Oh, so it's you who's trying to cause a panic here in town. I'll have you know I spoke to the director last night and he assured me he had you on a lease." "Excuse me?" Hank stopped her, "hold on everyone. Sir, if you could just give us five minutes of your time. I'm sure we can clear this all up." "Hold that call," the mayor shouted to the secretary. "You have three minutes starting now."

Hank and Renee told the mayor/judge, their story about the attacks and how the plague was starting to spread. "Where's your proof? Why hasn't the sheriff contacted me about these deaths or the hospital about this so-called plague?" "Well sir, the sheriff has the plague himself and was admitted to the hospital this morning." "Why hasn't the hospital called you? Why don't you call them? You have to cancel the fair and seal off this town," Renee screamed. "There are thousands of lives at stake here including your own." Hank cut in, "Sir, if you would just call the hospital I'm sure they will confirm what we just told you." "Fine, I will." The mayor had his secretary make the call. She dialed the number to the hospital when the head nurse answered she transferred the call to his office. "This is the mayor get me the chief of operations please." "Yes sir, please hold." In ten seconds she came back on the line Dr. Going's was on the phone.

"Hello, Mr. Mayor, what can I do for you today?" Going's was still in his car he had all incoming calls forwarded to his cell phone. "I'm going to put you on the speaker. I have a couple of concerned citizens here who seem to think there's some type of outbreak about to happen." Renee and Hank repeated what they knew and then it came. The cool calmness of Dr. Going, "I'm sorry," he said, "but we've received no reports of anything like that. There was one little boy brought in yesterday but he's fine. You did a great job of getting him to the hospital in the quick manner that you did, Mr. Peterson. He's resting now and we expect he'll be going home within the next twenty-hours." "There you have it," the mayor butted in, "sorry to bother you Doctor." "No problem Mr. Mayor, always willing to help but I do have a staff meeting to get to." "Mr. Peterson and Ms. Ward, goodbye," Going's hung up the phone. "There's something wrong here. This shit doesn't add up," Renee said. "Your three minutes are up. I have to insist you leave and being the Judge of this town if I hear one squeak of this craziness I'll have you both locked up. That's a promise now get out of my office!" Hank and Renee left, they tried to do things the right way but now it was time to play hardball.

Chapter 35

Alex Reed and his men were set up at motel 66 on route 99 not far from Spellman's house. Renee told him her concerns about Spellman. Not to mention, Volen Hughes had been tracking his work also. Alex Reed was well aware of the trouble and the potential danger Newton, Iowa was in for. He'd seen whole towns blown off the map while in the CIA and took part in similar types of destruction during Desert Storm. The time was now 11:00 am. The clock was ticking fast they only had four hours left to get the proof they needed to get the town sealed off and the rest of the CDC team in place. Renee called Alex, "are you in place?" "All set just waiting on your word pretty lady." Alfred and Thomas were stationed outside of Newton General waiting on Renee's call. It was time for Renee to put her plan in effect. She had briefed everyone earlier. She told Alex to wait for her call; then called Alfred. His phone rang twice and he picked up.

"Renee?" "Yes, Alfred it's me. Go ahead with the first sequence of the plan." "Got you, I'll call you in a few." Alfred looked at Thomas and gave him a nod. He pulled out a package and gave himself a shot. He injected himself with the flu. In fifteen minutes he would have all the flu symptoms as if he had the virus. He checked his wire as Thomas drove him up to the emergency entrance, took him inside and returned to the car. He was admitted right away and taken to the second floor where the other infected people where being held. He was told that a Doctor Spellman, would be in to check on him soon. That meant Spellman was indeed at the hospital. Alfred called, "Renee he's here." "Okay, you know what to do." "Yes." Renee called Alex back and told him to go ahead with the plan. Alex had one of his men drop him off about a hundred yards in back of Spellman's house off route 99. The highway was never used by anyone so they wouldn't be seen breaking into Spellman's house. Alex was an expert at these types of things. He would break in, plant bugs all around and look for the files. Renee planted a bug in the mayor's office so they could tune in. Alex's second man was back at motel 66. His job was to monitor all calls from Spellman and the mayor's cell phones. These were quite easy to tap into when you worked for the man who owned most of the wireless phone companies in the states. Hank hadn't read the note from the sheriff and decided now was a good time. He pulled the note from his pocket and began reading.

It said, "check out Spellman and Dr. Going's, trying to hide something. Go to shed in back of house the key is taped on back. Get my wife and son as well as your family out of Newton." Hank called home to check on his family. They were fine Ronda assured him. Alex made his way to Spellman's house and was disconnecting the alarm system. He pulled out his locksmith set and easily opened the door. "I'm in!" First, he planted bugs in the phones and other miscellaneous spots around the house. Then he began to search for the files. Nothing, he had searched the first two floors, turned up nothing and now was headed down to the cellar. In the cellar he found and took pictures of the files he found but these still were not the right ones. That's when he located the door. He tried it and it was locked. He called Renee from his wireless head set. "Do you read me?" "Yes, we're here Alex what do you have?" "Looks like some files from past experiments. I'm trying to get into what appears to be some type of secret door. I don't know where it leads. I need to have a look at those files right away Alex." "Gotcha," he replied, "pulling out in five, meet me at the 66." Alex was still working with the door when it finally opened.

He froze for a moment. The blue flashing lights started to blink he walked in and could see there was a long corridor. Dammit, he said to himself. I don't have time right now. I have to report these findings. I'll have to come back.

Chapter 36

Dr. Going arrived at the hospital and was being briefed by some of his staff when Spellman walked in. They were under the impression that the few people they had checked in had some type of flu-bug. "We're waiting for the results of some tests to be sent back to us from the CDC." "Good," Going said, "when the results get here notify me and me only. Until that information gets here I want you all to go about your daily duties. If anyone checks in with these flu like symptoms isolate them on the second floor. No one is to say a word to anyone outside this room especially the media. As you all know, the fair is tomorrow and we cannot risk panic over a little anthrax scare or a twenty-four hour flu bug. That will be all for now you're all excused." The staff got up and began to leave muttering to themselves. All except Lou Spellman, he stayed behind.

"Come with me," Going told Spellman as he rose from the head of the table. The two men went to his office. Alfred had stolen some hospital clothes and slipped into the meeting unnoticed. He had followed Going and Spellman to Going's office. They went in. Luckily there was a vacant office next door, so Alfred broke in and set up one of his listening devices. "How are you holding up son?' "Just fine a bit nervous but I'll be just fine." "And what about the sheriff?" "I gave him a shot of penicillin, turns out he's allergic to it. He'll have a reaction in about two hours and then he'll die. It's non-traceable." "Fine," Going took out his briefcase and pulled out the files they had found last night. "We need to get to your house. I'll get someone to look in after your patients. Our work is done here." "But, what about the squirrels," Spellman asked? "Don't worry son we'll deal with them tonight. Meet me at your house in an hour." Going grabbed his briefcase and the two men left. Alfred overheard it all. "My God!" Going and Spellman had just passed the office Alfred was in when Alfred bumped into the desk. Going kept walking but

Spellman stopped. "What is it?" "I thought I heard something." "Yeah, you're right you and everyone else in this fucking hospital. Let's go." Going started walking again. Spellman stood still looking at the empty office. He stuck his hand out toward the doorknob. He was just about to try and open it. Alfred pulled out his gun. He had forgotten to lock the door back behind him. Spellman had his hand on the doorknob now and was about to twist it when he felt a hand on his shoulder. It was Going, "now," Going, said, "let's go right now we don't have time for this shit." Spellman released the knob and walked away with Going and a feeling, something or someone was in that room. They both left the hospital but not together.

Alfred stayed for a brief moment, called Renee and told her what had happen. Hank and Renee were both with Alex when she got the call from Alfred. He was on the speaker so they all heard his report. Hank shouted, "Going, that's it, that's what was in the sheriff's note. We have to get over to the hospital and help him." "Sorry, no can do," Alex said. "Renee it's your call." "Hank, I'm deeply sorry it's to late for the sheriff," Renee told him. "Here let me see that note." As Renee read the note, Alex told Alfred to search Going's office and get back up to his hospital room before they started to look for him. "Hank," Renee said, "we can't save the sheriff but we can try and get his family out." Renee passed Alex the note and told her man to get the sheriff's family out of there and meet them at the motel so she could begin real treatments. "You got it," Alfred asked? She told Thomas to trail Going to Spellman's house without getting noticed. "Got it?" Goings walked out, went to his car and pulled out of the lot slowly. Thomas was not far behind.

"Renee," Alex said, "I think it's time for you to pull your men out and let my guys take over." "You're right." Alfred had already broken too many laws and she knew this thing wasn't over yet. "Okay, have one of your men take over for Thomas and follow Going." Hank cut in, "but how is he going to do that if Thomas is already in route?" "Don't worry, Mr. Peterson it's not a problem." "Hank," Renee said, "as soon as Alfred and Thomas get here we need to get your family and the sheriff's family out of Newton. I'll have Alfred and Thomas take them. It's the only way."

Two hours had passed and Renee still didn't have the proof she needed to seal off the town and stop the fair. It would take at least four hours to get the samples from the squirrel killings to Atlanta and analyzed. This was turning into a real mess. They had to stop the plague from spreading, track down and kill all the squirrels that were spreading it. She knew if the CDC out of Atlanta wasn't in charge then they would bring in Chris Jenkins.

Chapter 37

Alfred had just arrived he had gotten the sheriff's family out. Mrs. Brown was crying hysterically. She knew her husband had been killed. Their son Casey was asleep. "How could this happen?" She was screaming and sobbing at the same time. "They knew he was allergic to penicillin." Renee took her to the couch and tried to comfort her. She gave her and Casey the necessary shots and something to put them to sleep. "Let's hear that tape," Renee told Alfred, "but first get Bear on the horn."

"Bear, I believe I got the proof we need for you to send in the rest of the team and seal this town off." "Renee, I'm sorry but it's too late." "I don't understand, Sir listen to this tape it clearly proves they are lying trying to hide something. I can have the samples to you in less than three hours." "Sorry Renee." "No sir, just listen to this tape." Before Bear could stop her from playing the tape she had started it. Now it was truly too late. Everyone was silent while the tape played. Then it ended and Renee spoke, "you see Sir, we have all we need." That's when a strange voice came over the speaker.

"Ms. Ward, this is Chris Jenkins of the US Army Disease Control Unit." "Fuck", Alex said loudly. Renee turned and stared at him. "Who was that Ms. Ward?" "Bear what is he doing there?" "Well, Ms Ward let me answer that for you. Under article six twenty-two you are required to submit and report all findings of any type of crossbreeding or cloning attempts that you come across. It seems you left your findings here in Atlanta and you know they have to be reported to us directly. Remember the CDC is part of the government but I'll tell you what I'm going to do. My team is already in route to Newton. They should arrive around seven in the morning. You and your team are to pull out now, bring me all of your findings and we'll handle the rest." Alex could no longer hold his silence. "Fuck Jenkins, no! You mean you're prepared to nuke the whole town don't you dear friend?" Bear jumped back into the conversation. "Who is that and Renee what's going on?" "It's Alex, Alex Reed," Jenkins said. "You people are way out of line involving a civilian in this. I should have you all locked up. Mr. Russell, you have six hours to get me what I asked for and get your people out of Newton. I have a job to do. As for you Alex, you better be long gone when I get there because if you're not, you're going down."

"I gather he's an old friend, Sir?" Bear knew she was right but his hands were tied there was nothing he could do to stop Jenkins now. It was out of their hands. "You heard the man," Bear said, "pull out now and that's an order." "Dammit Alex, what was that all about what are you doing?" Renee demanded to know. "Listen to me people and listen good, make no mistake about what is about to happen to this town. Your plan was good Renee but now we have no time left."

Alex told them about how Volen Hughes had financed Lisa Straub years ago and of her marriage to Dr. Jackson. He explained how they had failed miserably with their experiments in Asia. And, how they had gotten the baby out of Asia before he could become infected with the plague with the help of a one, Dr. Going. It was all starting to make sense now, Hank and Renee thought to themselves. "Well what can we do," Hank asked? "I'm not going to ask you to stay behind Mr. Peterson; you need to get your family out of here. Renee you have to get your people out of here too including yourself." "No way Alex, if I hadn't left the samples then we wouldn't be in this situation." "Not true, every time a potential infectious disease is tested the government knows about it. Remember who pays the bills. They're not going to be left out." "Fine, I'm still not leaving. Can we talk in the other room?" "Sure, Hank I would like for you to join us." "Okay." Renee, Hank and Alex went into the next room.

Once in the room Alex laid out his plan telling them they had to get the Genetic Mutation files that Going was no doubt holding. Hank was to go to the sheriff's house and see exactly what was in the shed. Renee would get her people out of town with the Peterson's and the sheriff's family. Alex and his two men would pay a visit to Dr. Spellman's house and see exactly where the door led. Alex's man had been outside of Spellman's house that's where he followed Going. "Get back over here ASAP he told his man." "Sure thing but both of them are in the house right now. This Going fellow just pulled up and the other Doc let him in." "Well Alex, what now," Renee asked? "We go as planned nothing changes," Alex told them. "Keep your headsets and phone lines clear." "What about the squirrels," Hank asked? "I'm not worried about them right now, Mr. Peterson. Right now we have to get as many people out of this town as possible. The squirrels will be killed when Jenkins nukes the town and trust me he is going to nuke this town no matter how many innocent people he kills in the process. You see the problem is just as you feared Renee. This town has been infected with the Plague, which he's not going to try to contain or treat. And you have these mutated squirrels that the Feds have to cover up, eliminate and deny all knowledge of their existence." "So," Hank asked, "you mean the government is going to cover up the truth?" "You got it, now we need not waste any more time. Are you two staying or going?"

Chapter 38

Hank and Alfred went to the sheriff's house to search the shed. Thomas would meet them at Hank's house. Alex and his men went back over to Spellman's house while Renee stayed at the motel to monitor calls and keep watch over the sheriff's family. Hank called his mother and told her to meet him at his house within the hour. He just didn't know how he was going to tell Ronda that he would be staying. It was three o'clock, although Renee had pulled out all the stops she had failed to get the job done. She felt responsible for what was now inevitable to happen to the people of Newton, Iowa. She knew it was still an uphill battle. How were they going to warn people? Make them understand the danger they were in and not get killed or locked up in the process.

A little red light came on one of Alex's monitoring stations. Someone was calling Spellman's house. She hit the button. "Alex, are you getting this?" "Got it, just hold tight." "Hello." "Yes, this is the mayor, Doctor, I was told I could catch Doctor Going there." "Just a second," Spellman said. "Dr. Going, it's for you," he said as he passed him the phone. Now Renee and Alex both thought to themselves, this should be interesting. How was the mayor connected to all of this? "Going?" "Yes, it's me where are you?" "I'm about ten minutes away." "Fine hurry, we have lots to discuss." "Doctor, are you sure about Spellman?" "He's fine now did you do as I instructed?" "Yes." "Well then we'll see you when you get here," Going said and hung up the phone. "The mayor," Spellman asked, "what's he got to do with this and why is he coming over here?" "Because like you and me he's knee deep in this shit and the three of us are going to see it all the way to the end."

That was it now Renee and Alex understood what had happen. Alex and his men could do nothing but wait and listen. He didn't dare storm the house and risk not getting hold to what Volen Hughes, really wanted. He would have to wait until they left even if it took all day. Hank and Alfred arrived at the sheriff's house and proceeded to the back toward the shed. It was just like the sheriff described in his note. A key was taped to the back of the shed near the bottom. Hank grabbed the key and opened the lock. He slid the doors open and the two men stood in amazement. Inside the shed was enough weapons and artillery to arm a small army. Hank wondered what it was all for? Why would the sheriff of a small town have all that ammunition? He called Renee and Alex. "I'm in, there's enough shit in here to wage your own private little war." "That's great," Alex, said, "get all you can we're going to need it. Be sure to get some bulletproof vests if there's any there. Don't waste a lot of time. Get the stuff, head to your house and get your family out Hank," Renee said. "Thomas," she said, "time for you to go. Take the sheriff's family meet Hank at his house you and Alfred drive everyone up to Des Moines. Then hop a plane to Detroit once you get them there you and Alfred take the connecting flight to Atlanta. Thomas, make sure everyone gets on the plane. Oh and give this package to Bear. Don't open it, good luck." She gave him a hug and said goodbye.

Thomas took the sheriff's family loaded them into the van and left. Hank and Alfred took all they could load including the vests and headed for his house. As Alex sat in the van waiting he dozed off, started having dreams about what happened years ago when he and Jenkins were both assigned to the desert storm project.

Chapter 39

(Flashback)

Alex Reed and Chris Jenkins had been the best of friends. They had gone though boot camp together at a very young age. Both were on the fast track to the top as far as the military. Then they got the call assigning them to operation desert storm in Iraq. They put Chris in charge of unit 22 and Alex second in command. The Iraq's had been charged with storing biochemical warheads in a small town just south of Baghdad. Their mission was to destroy all warheads no matter what the cost. Chris Jenkins had his orders and was determined to carry them out at all cost. He didn't tell anyone in his unit what those orders were. He informed them it was confidential and that they would learn things on a need to know basis. Alex being his friend went along with it and helped rally the rest of the men's support.

Chris and Alex were both tired, at about 1:00 am Iraq's time the call came. The orders were to take out a small village believed to be storing and shipping warheads. It was late and the men were all tired. Just as Chris was receiving the message the lines of communication went down for about thirty seconds. Chris swore he had got the correct location. Alex questioned him about the information. Chris pulled out his gun, pointed it at Alex's head and told him if he ever second-guessed him again or failed to follow a direct order he would blow his brains out. He wouldn't have to worry about a court-martial. They bombed the wrong village and thousands of innocent people were killed meaninglessly. After that, Alex finished his tour of duty and joined the CIA. Chris Jenkins went on to become a captain and was now in charge of the US Army Disease Control Unit. Alex woke up and looked at his watch. He also knew he would have to stop Chris Jenkins once and for all.

Chapter 40

Hank and Alfred pulled up to Hank's house. This part was going to be tough Hank thought. Thomas had already arrived and Ronda was in the doorway along with Miko. Hank looked up at the roof and saw that the squirrels had returned. He dare not move to fast and didn't want to alarm the others. The two men made it into the house without any problems. JP and the rest of the family including the sheriff's wife and son were there too. Ronda, JP and Miko rushed him. "Hank what the hell is going on?" "Just hold on and take a seat now listen. Listen very carefully I'm going to tell you what I know. I'm going to tell you what you all are going to do. That's what has to be done period no questions asked." Hank knew this approach was not going to work but he had to start somewhere.

There would be questions and lots of them. He introduced Alfred and Thomas first. He needed their expertise and back up.

He explained the story of Josh and Lisa Straub, as he knew it. He described how it related to what was happening now and the danger they faced. Not just them but the whole community of Newton, Iowa. Then he told them how much he loved them and would sacrifice everything for them. "You have to get out of here," he told them. "And you Hank," his wife and mother said, "what about you? What are you going to do save the fucking town? Save the world? We need you too. You need to save yourself not others." Miko put her two cents in too. "Fuck this shit sis, I'm out of here! Al, Tom, whoever you guys are, give me ten minutes. You can take me and the kids to the airport," Miko told them. JP and the sheriff's wife agreed they were getting out too. "Alright dammit," Ronda said, "let me call Porter and Tash's people to tell them to get out of here too." Hank grabbed his wife hugged her, kissed her and told her he would be fine. He would join them in Detroit in 36 hours at the most. After all, he didn't have a death wish but Hank did feel responsible in some small way. "There's one more thing," Hank said, "I noticed some squirrels on the roof so we must move swiftly and cautiously. Alfred, Thomas, get them to Des Moines and on that plane safely." "You got it friend but how do we get pass the squirrels," Thomas asked? "Alright, we have twelve people not counting me and four vehicles we should be able to get six in each truck. I'll drive the third one. One is in the garage so that shouldn't be a problem. The other one is right outside the garage and two on the curb. Thomas you take Miko, Shannon, JP, Casey and Mrs. Brown with you. Take the vehicle in the garage. Alfred you take my wife, Jasmine, Terrez, Porter and Tash with you. I'll create some sort of distraction so I can get to the van on the curb while you get into the other truck with my family." "Hank, what type of distraction," Ronda asked? "You know those clothes you were going to give to the Salvation Army?" "Yes," she said, "get them, all of them. Alfred, Thomas didn't Alex say he was sure Jenkins was going to nuke the town?" "Yes he did," Alfred said. "Then nukes cause fire correct," Hank asked? "True, but what's your point?" "I have at lease five gallons of gasoline in the garage. I was planning on doing some yard work. If we make some torches it should be enough to get everyone to the trucks and hold off the squirrels, right?" "Yes it should be Mr. Peterson," Thomas and Alfred agreed. Hank tied the clothes around some old pool table sticks he had in the garage and soaked them with gasoline. You could hear the squirrels gnawing on the roof. The children were getting scared. Hank lit the torches and everyone got into the vehicles while he ran to the truck in front. The squirrels didn't even try to attack. It was as if they were waiting on something special. He climbed in and watched Thomas and Alfred drive off with his family. He wondered how he'd get out of town.

Chapter 41

Renee was listening in on the conversation between the three men when Hank walked in. “What’s going on,” he asked? “They’re planning on leaving town right during the fair tomorrow,” Renee said. “But, what about Jenkins do they know what he has planned for the town?” “No, I don’t think they know, Alex what do you think?” “I’m going to deal with Jenkins we’ll find out exactly when he plans to nuke the town and try to stop it.” Alex was still listening from the van to the three men. “Hank did you get everything from the shed?” “All we could carry,” Hank replied. “Okay, I’m going to head back over there and see what we’ve got. Time is running out I’ll leave one of my men here.” He left one of his men and instructed him to call as soon as the three men left the house. He had to get that file and see where that room with the blinking lights lead. Going told the mayor to attend the fair. He and Spellman would meet him at noon on the fairground. Then they would drive to the Mayor's office and take the mayor's private helicopter. "Fine," the mayor left and Alex walked in the door. That's when they heard it. "What about the squirrels at the hospital," Spellman asked? "Tonight we'll go to the hospital and torch them. We'll use the tunnel that way no one will see us and by the time they put the fire out there will be nothing left." "What tunnel," Hank asked? "What squirrels at the hospital," Renee said? "Wait a minute my wife's sister said that there were a lot of strange animal like noises coming from the sixth floor of the hospital. In fact, she said it was one of the labs up there, lab 621. No one uses that floor she said but there was something going on up there." "Okay, but what tunnel?" "I think I know now," Alex said. "In Spellman's house in the basement I found this door it has to be the tunnel. There were these strange blinking lights and a long corridor. I didn't get to the end." Alex headed for the door, "Mr. Peterson let's have a look at what you got from the shed. Renee stay tuned and see if you can find out anything else."

Hank and Alex went outside to the van. Hank opened the back door and Alex stood and stared for a moment. Then he hopped in the back, started going threw the piles and stacks of weapons Hank brought back. That's when he saw what he was looking for. "Great," he said to himself and hopped out the van. The two men went back inside. "Okay people listen up this is what we have to do. Hank and Renee, I need you two to go to the fair and warn people that they have to get out of town. I'm sure they will be making announcements over the loud speaker so you'll have to get a hold of the mike. Once you've warned the people head for Des Moines. You're going to have to take some weapons with you. I'm sure you'll run into some resistance. My men and I will try to stop Jenkins." "What about the mayor and the doctors," Hank asked? "What about the squirrel's," Renee added. "How do we stop them?" "I don't know but we have to try and stop Jenkins from nuking this town. We'll have to find a way to deal with the squirrels later." "What about their plan to burn up the hospital," Hank asked? "I don't believe they're planning on burning down the whole hospital just whatever is up in that lab. I'll be there tonight to try and stop them." There was a knock on the door. Alex pulled out his gun and asked, "anyone expecting company?" Everyone nodded no. Alex headed for the door snatched it open and pulled the woman inside who was standing there. He put the gun to her head and shouted, "who are you and what are you doing here?" "No Alex," Hank screamed. "It's my wife. Ronda what are you doing here?" "I, she started to say, "we couldn't just leave you here." "We," Hank shouted, "who else is with you?" Jasmine, Terrez, Porter, and Tash walked in. "Oh my God," Renee said, as she took a seat. "Ronda where are the rest of them? I told Thomas to make sure everyone got on the plane." "He tried, Ms. Ward but I had to resist. Hank your mom, Miko, Shannon, the sheriff's family and those two men all got on the plane." "And you should have too!" "Well," Alex said, "it's too late now. Mr. Peterson you're in charge of the safety for your family, so take them with you tomorrow to the fair nothing changes." Alex's walkie-talkie went off. "Alex…come in." "I read you Cecil what is it?" Cecil was one of Alex's men the one watching the house. "They are leaving," Cecil told Alex. "Did anyone hear them say where they were going?" "No," Cecil and Renee both answered. "Alright, hold tight I'll be there in a few minutes. I'm heading back to Spellman's house. We need to find the package. Hank you said your wife's sister worked at the hospital." "Yes," Hank replied, "but she got on the plane." "Mrs. Peterson, do you know anyone else who works at the hospital?" "Just her friend Mike but he seems to have disappeared." "Damn!" "Why do you ask?" "We need about six pints of blood." "Blood, what for," Renee asked? "I don't have time to explain now." "Well," Hank said, "there is a blood bank about fifteen miles out of town." "Then you have to go now. Take Craig with you no less than six pints. Also stop and get some freezer bags and pizza." "Pizza?" "Yes, at lease three large ones. It's going to be a long night and you appear to have mouths to feed, Mr. Peterson. When you two get back no one leaves, no one gets in. Am I clear?" "Yes," they all said. "Renee keep listening, Jenkins is no fool he'll be looking for anything out of the ordinary. You have to hurry I'm sure he's going to place his men on all borders of town." Alex left and just as Hank and Craig were about to leave Terrez came out of the back room. "Daddy," he said. "Yes, Terrez what is it?" "Watch out for the squirrels." "I promise I will," Hank said and the two men left.

Chapter 42

Renee wondered why Hank's wife had really returned. Was she jealous? Did she suspect that Renee had feelings for her husband or was she just plain stupid? Why would she endanger the lives of her children? Renee had to know. Ronda was on her way to the room with the kids when Renee said, "Mrs. Peterson can we talk for a minute?" "Sure, what would you like to talk about?" "Well, first do you still have the vaccines for the children?" "Yes, of course I do." "Ronda, if I may call you that, why did you come back here? Don't you understand the danger you've put yourself and your children in?" "Of course I understand but do you understand that, that's my husband and these are his children? We are a family so we're here to help, not get in the way. You see when this is all over we still plan on being a family. I also see the way you look at him." "Well Ms. Peterson, you do have an attractive intelligent man but my purpose here is to try to save this town and it's people, nothing else." "Then Renee Ward, we don't have a problem. I'm willing to put all this behind us and try to help the people of Newton, Iowa and save our own ass' at the same time," Ronda said as she struck out her hand. "Deal," Renee said and shook her hand.

Chapter 43

Hank and Craig headed for the blood bank. It was around 7:00 pm, they knew the bank would be closed. Hank asked, "Craig how are we going to get in?" "Don't worry when you work for Alex Reed access is not a problem." "How far is it?" "Not far, about twenty minutes down the highway." What on earth could he want with six pints of blood Hank wondered? Going and Spellman were headed for the hospital when Going said, "turn around I left my briefcase." Alex was in the house he hadn't seen the briefcase he was in the tunnel and the lights were blinking. "Alex," his walkie- talkie went off, "get out of there. You're going to have company in about one minute," Cecil said. Alex turned and ran for the door. He got out and shut the door just in time. The two men were coming down the stairs. "Where did you leave it," Spellman asked? "There it is over there." Renee and Ronda were listening to all this back at the room. Alex thought about jumping the two men. He had his gun out and was hiding behind the furnace. Just before he was about to make his move the phone upstairs rang. This gave him a few more minutes to contemplate his actions. What if they didn't have the files on them? What if they were at the hospital? He would have to stick with his plan and get them tomorrow when they were going to leave town. They would surely have them then. Spellman ran upstairs to get the phone and Going was right behind him. "Hello," Spellman answered the phone. "Hello…," no answer Renee just held the line. Spellman hung the phone up and a few minutes later the two men left the house again. "All clear," Cecil said. Renee and Ronda both let out a deep breath. "Alex that was to close…get out of there!" "Not yet, I'm going to see where this tunnel leads, give me ten minutes." Alex headed back into the tunnel and down the cold path with the blinking lights. As he got closer to the end of the tunnel he heard it. The gnawing, it had to be the squirrels. The noise got louder and louder and he wondered if they could get out. He came right to the door, reached down to open it and stopped. It sounded like hundreds and hundreds of squirrels could be behind that door. Why would he open it anyway? He pulled his hand back turned away from the door and left.

Hank and Craig pulled around to the back of the little building that served as Newton's blood bank reserve. Most blood was kept in the hospital but they always had a special reserve in case of an emergency. Hank remembered Miko talking about it once. Craig got out of the truck, went to the back of the building and started fumbling around with wires. "What are you doing," Hank said? "I have to cut the alarm just look out and make sure no one comes up." After what seemed to be an hour to Hank, Craig finally spoke. "Okay, I cut the alarm give me five more minutes just keep watch." Hank did so but they were being watched also. A small gathering of squirrels was in the nearby tree peering at the two men. Hank was starting to get nervous. He felt as though something bad was going to happen. Something touched his shoulder and he jumped. He turned around, "come on. Are you all right? Looks like you've seen a ghost," Craig said. The two men loaded the blood in the back hopped in and left while the squirrels continued to watch. Hank and Craig had been on the road for about ten minutes when they saw the military vehicles heading for the outskirts of town. "Keep your cool and keep driving," Craig said. The men had on masks and gloves as if to protect them from some type of germ. The plague, no doubt about ten trucks passed in all. One truck stopped about twenty yards ahead of them. "Dammit, they're setting up a roadblock. Just keep calm slow down and see what they want," Craig said. Craig had his gun close he was not going to be taken in. Hank stopped the van and rolled down the window. "What seems to be the problem?" "This road is off limits. Where are you coming from and where are you going?" "We're heading to Newton General. We have to get them some blood. There was a bad accident earlier and the hospital was low on blood type B positive. Here would you like to see," Hank asked? "No, that won't be necessary but I do need you to open the back. There's no one back there is it?" "No sir, just us two." Hank got out and opened the back doors. The enlisted man took a quick peak and told him to go ahead. "Just like I said sir, just delivering this much needed blood." Hank got back in the van, just as he was about to pull off the young man stopped him. "Wait a second," he pulled out a photo, "have either of you seen this man?" Hank and Craig looked at the picture both shrugged and said, "no." "Okay, take it with you. If you happen to see this man call the number on the bottom." "We sure will," Hank said. The young man stepped back hopped into his truck, drove off and Hank did the same. "Fuck!" Alex shouted he was back at the room with Renee, Ronda, Cecil and the kids. They had all been listening though Craig's walkie-talkie. "Let me guess, it's a picture of me right," Alex said? "You got it and I must add not a good one. Okay you have about five minutes to get off that road and dump that truck." "Where and how do we get back to you," Craig replied? Hank cut in, "we could park it at my dealership. We're only five minutes from there. I can get us another truck or van." "Great, Mr. Peterson head over there and park that one out of sight. Call us before you leave your dealership because we may have to relocate from here. I'll know for sure in twenty minutes. Cecil, get me that frequency Jenkins and his boys are on now." "I'm working on it as we speak boss," Cecil told him. "What does this all mean," Ronda asked? "It means Jenkins knows I'm still here and he's probably got the whole state National Guards after me. It also means he's sealing off the town. Nobody else comes in and nobody, if he gets his way will leave." The guardsmen started setting up roadblocks and sealing off the back borders of the town. They passed the blood bank. It was only about five miles from where they set up. The young officer caught up with the rest of his group. He got out of his truck, walked up to a tall lanky man, "Private Farr reporting, sir." "Report," the tall man said. "Sir, I stopped the truck as you ordered. There were only two men in the truck, sir. No one resembled the man in the photo, sir." "Private Farr, where were they coming from?" "The blood bank, sir, they said there had been an accident in town and the hospital was low on blood, sir." "Private, did you by any chance notice when you just drove by that the goddam blood bank…that it's closed?" "Yes sir but I thought." The tall flaky man was furious now. His name was Sergeant Avery. "DID I ASK YOU TO THINK PRIVATE?" "No sir," the private mumbled. "I ASKED YOU TO STOP THEM. DETAIN THEM AND CALL ME PRIVATE. IS THAT CORRECT PRIVATE?" "Yes sir." "Then what in the fuck were you thinking? Don't you know I could have you shot for disobeying a direct order? GET BACK TO YOUR UNIT AND YOUR SORRY ASS OUT MY FACE. Private Steel get me Captain Jenkins on the horn now."

"Ten minutes Cecil I need it now. Hold on sir something's coming over now." "Jenkins here," Alex could hear him now. "Captain Jenkins this is Private Steel I have Sergeant Avery for you sir." Alex looked up at Ronda and Renee. "Get out of here, take the kids, leave now hurry. Cecil get them loaded and come back and help me with this shit. We have ten minutes people move! Renee just get on the road I'll call you." "Captain Jenkins this is Sergeant Avery. We stopped two men in a van claiming to be delivering blood to the hospital from the blood bank." "Do you have those men in your custody now Sergeant?" "No sir, one of my privates let them slip through his fingers." "How long ago," Sergeant Jenkins demanded? "Eight minutes then get your people on that road and find that van, check every motel, nook and cranny, on that highway. Find those two men and detain them Sergeant. Is that clear? I'll be there by five in the morning I just got off the phone with the pentagon and this is a priority one operation. Do you understand?" "Yes sir, Captain." Renee, Ronda and the kids were speeding down the highway. Alex and Cecil loaded the rest of their equipment in the truck. “Five minutes until they reach us let’s go,” Alex shouted. Alex and Cecil sped down the highway in the opposite direction. You could see the dust settling and the tire marks. Two trucks of guardsman pulled up to the motel. Ten armed men got out and went from room to room. Nothing, they came across the room in the back, the motel office. You could hear sounds coming from inside. They bust in the door searched the place, “nothing sir.” One of the privates said to Sergeant Avery, “we must have just missed them.” Sergeant Avery, shot the TV, “let’s go men on the double they can’t be to far ahead of us. Private Steel, get me the base I need a chopper in the air now.” Steel made the call to the base. “Ten minutes sir, that’s what they say to airborne time. They’re fueling now.” “Give me that phone this is a priority one operation get that bird in the air now.” “Yes sir,” the voice on the other side of the phone said. “What are we looking for?” “A white van, possibly two, do not intercept just keep me posted of their location.” “Mr. Peterson we need a place to put up,” Alex was saying into the walkie-talkie. “We can go to my mother’s house.”

Alex called, "Renee head for Peterson's mother's house. You have five minutes until they're airborne," he said. "Ronda how far?" "Turn here off the highway it's about six minutes from this exit." Although, Renee and Ronda were in the jeep they still didn't want to be spotted on the highway. "Hank you and Craig head over there now." "We're still on the highway. Where do we get off at, we're coming up on exit 13, Alex shouted." "That's it exit west and go to exit six," Hank said. Sergeant Avery and his two truckloads of men were just about to leave the motel when Private Steel said, "Sir, I think you should have a look at this, sir." "What is it private, everyone load up they can't be too far ahead of us?"

That's when the first squirrel attacked. Within seconds, hundreds of squirrels covered the men some flying and some on the ground. Shots were being fired everywhere. A couple of men shot each other. Sergeant Avery and two privates managed to get back into the motel with just a couple of bites. But, they could hear the other men screaming in pain and horror as they were being torn apart. It was quiet after about ten minutes of the gnawing on live human flesh and the moaning from the seven men that didn't make it. "What just happen out there Sergeant?" The three men were in a state of shock and the phone was ringing. The Sergeant snapped out of it. He grabbed the phone. "You guys okay down there?" "What the hell was that, a voice said?" It was the two men in the chopper they had heard the screaming and flown to that location. But, they were too late. All they saw were piles of blood and bodies that had been mutilated by some type of animal. There were lots of dead squirrels lying around too. All seemed clear and quiet so Sergeant Avery opened the door and poked his head out. He started choking on his own vomit. One of the privates sat him down. He was okay after a few minutes and went outside. The chopper was still sitting in the middle of the highway. The pilot seeing the sergeant approaching got out the chopper and headed toward him. "Let's get you out of here, sir." The three men loaded up in the chopper. They were still in shock. "Where to sir," the pilot asked? "Private call the others and see if they're alright." "Yes sir Sergeant Avery," one of the privates moaned. The other men were fine nothing had happen there. Alex and Cecil were still tuned into Jenkins' channel and had heard the screaming and shooting. Jenkins had broken communication and went to a more secured channel. He figured Alex would be trying to listen. Alex and Cecil pulled up at JP's house and went inside with the other's. For the moment, everyone in the group was okay. Alex knew Jenkins would be in town tonight if he was not already. It was the same as before he never told the truth. He told you what you needed on a need to know basis. They unpacked the vans and jeep. Then ordered pizza in and had a meeting, the last stand you might call it. The kids were even in the meeting but now none of them had a choice. Ronda didn't like the children being involved. Hank told her they were going to need all the help they could get and it was alright in that house. "The freezer bags, we have to have the bags," Alex said. "I'll go there's a 7-eleven right around the corner," Cecil said.

Chapter 44

Jenkins was in town. He set up base about forty miles from Newton. Sergeant Avery was with him and his men were all in place. Jenkins had stationed men about fifty or so at every entrance and exit of the town. He was not going to chance these rookies blowing his operation. He knew his men were loyal to him. He called Bear Russell back to see if Renee and her men had returned and given up the files. "Negative," Bear told him unwillingly. The two men had returned but the files were not the right ones and Renee was AWOL. Jenkins ordered Bear to tell him everything he knew. Bear having no choice but to face jail time did so. He had given Renee a direct order. After that brief conversation, Jenkins ordered a few of his men to gather the mayor and bring him to the base.

They found the mayor in his office with his cock stuck up in one of the young townswomen. They put a gun to his head and suggested he come along quietly. They shot the young women in the head and took the mayor to the base. Jenkins poured him a drink and gave him a cigar. "Now, Mister Mayor, let me offer you a piece of advice. I'm going to ask you a few questions you're going to answer them. Not with I don't knows or any of your political bullshit. If you chose to give me a bullshit answer I will stab you right in your nuts. Drink up Mister Mayor. Sam, light his cigar." Sam lit the cigar and the mayor downed his whole drink. He was shaking like a leaf. "Alright Mister Mayor, here we go. Tell me everything you know about this plague, Dr. Going, Dr. Spellman and what are their plans?" The mayor told him everything he knew from the stocks to what was in the files and how much money it was worth. He also assured him that he could get him a big chunk of the money for sparing his life. "How touching but where are the files," Jenkins asked? "Going has them. He and Spellman should be at the hospital right now." "Sam, take two men with you and go get them." "Right away sir," Sam replied as he immediately left.

"Drink up," Jenkins said as he poured the mayor another drink.

Jenkins left the room but stationed two men with the mayor. "Get me the pentagon," he told one of his men. "Sir, I have General Cross on the line." "Thank you, that will be all." "Okay Jenkins, spit it out what's happening down there." "Well sir, I've sealed the town. They are under attack by some type of mutated squirrels that carry the plague. We have no known cure or vaccine for this type of plague." "Then what do you recommend Captain Jenkins?" "I recommend that we go ahead with project 2TLNB, sir." "There's no other way captain?" "No sir, the squirrels and the plague are already out of control." "What caused this captain?" "I'll have the files in less than an hour, sir." "Okay Captain, you have your duty what else do you need from me?" "Sir, I need a BLACKHAWK, down here ASAP. We'll launch from the blackhawk, destroying and freezing every living organism within a thirty-mile radius." "How many casualties are we taking captain?" "Well, General with the fair being tomorrow my guess is at least," he paused, "Five Thousand, at tops sir." "Captain, that the country can live with. What we can't live with is word of this getting out. Get the files on every resident in that town so we can personally contact there loved ones and clean this mess up." "Yes sir, I have the mayor with me right now and he has promised me his full cooperation." "Good the BlackHawk will be there at seven am with "TWO TONS OF LIQIUD NITROGEN BOMBS" (2TLNB)." "Thank you sir," Captain Jenkins said as he hung up the phone. Liquid Nitrogen he said to himself everything would freeze burn and crumble to death. There would be nothing left but ashes of all living things. Non-traceable perfect he said to himself he would launch them at 1:00 pm. The two tons would cover only a thirty-mile area. The BlackHawk could cover the other ten miles in about a minute. All the troops would be safe. He would have the files, Going and Spellman as prisoners/new partners. He would be a rich man, no more, yes sir. He would get out a rich man and fake his death.

Sam and his men walked Going and Spellman out the hospital with guns in their backs. They were at the base fifteen minutes later. "What's the meaning of this?" "Oh, I think you have a pretty good idea Dr. Going's right? Or are you Dr. Spellman? Nevertheless your good friend the mayor and I, have a business proposal for you that I'm sure you won't refuse. Sam, don't be rude to our newfound friends. I mean newfound partners pour them a drink and give them a cigar." "You're no friend of mine and whatever your proposal is I'll just assume pass right now." Jenkins slapped Spellman and pushed him on the floor. "Get him up Sam! How dare you not accept my hospitality," Jenkins said through clenched teeth! "Did you think what you were doing would go unnoticed? Do you think we're fools, terrorist or some bullshit. I stand here with the greatest authority on this planet. How dare you interrupt me! You little fucking weasel. Sure you may save a few lives, but I save the world. Cut him Sam so we're sure not to have any more doubt about my offer." Two men grabbed Spellman sat him at the table and cut off his pinky finger. When he screamed they shoved a rag in his mouth. "Do I have your attention now gentlemen Jenkins shouted? Drink up Doc it will help the pain.

Now we have been watching your research and your fathers for the last thirty years. It's out of control but I understand you two have finally got it right. Tomorrow this town will be no more. We will all leave together and corner the market on your newfound wealth. I don't see that as being unfair since I'm going to let you live do you?" "Not a problem there's more than enough for everyone." "Good. That's what I want to hear. You two need me as much as I need you so let's have another drink and discuss tomorrow." Going was calm he knew no one could do anything without him. He had notes and formulas stored in his head. They didn't dare injure him. "Well, let's get down to it," Going said. "I mean if you're going to nuke the town we want to be well on our way." Going pulled up a seat, lit a cigar and took a drink. "Ready," he asked? "Ready," Jenkins said as he too pulled up a seat.

Going told them about the squirrels in the hospital and how they planned to torch them tonight. "The good doctor and I here will still do that but we have to get back to the hospital. We have to be seen just in case something goes wrong before you nuke the town in the morning." "Fine," Jenkins said. "By the way where are the files Going," Jenkins asked? "Well partner like you said we all need each other. So when we're out of here you get to see the files. One more thing Captain, I don't need my man disfigured anymore." "Fine, I'll have my men help put out the fire at the hospital. Also Dr. Spellman anything of value you need out of your house I suggest you get it. It too is going up in flames. Mr. Mayor you stay with us I'll have a couple of the boys go by your house and get you some fresh things for your farewell speech to Newton tomorrow. Sam give them their keys, you brought their car here right?" "Yes sir." "Well you two are free to go. I look forward to the fireworks. Sam bandage up our good Dr. Spellman's hand, he's bleeding like a pig, oh and give him his finger back. I'm sure the good doctor's can still save it." Everyone but Jenkins, Sergeant Avery and the mayor left the room.

Sergeant Avery was scared his National Guard training had not prepared him for anything like this. "Requesting permission to speak Captain Jenkins, Sir." "What is it Sergeant?" "Sir, I wondered if I might be able to get in touch with my family? Some of them stay in town." "Of course Sergeant, please have them come to the designated area tonight." "Thank you captain." "May I use your phone?" "Of course Sergeant help yourself." Sergeant Avery picked up the phone. There was a loud noise and Sergeant Avery hit the floor. Jenkins had blown his brains out from the back of his head. “Very disobedient man,” Jenkins said to the mayor. “Can’t seem to get his orders right. I wonder how he ever made Sergeant?” Jenkins left the room and went to the other side of the base. Sam placed a bug in Spellman’s wrapping so that they would be able to hear any plans of a double-cross. “Anything yet Sam,” Jenkins asked? “No sir, not yet, they’re just coming out the restroom and leaving the base.” “Good, keep listening if you hear anything I should know about wake me. I’m going to grab a few zees and dream about my good friend Alex. Wake me when the fireworks start.” “Yes sir you got it.”

As Going and Spellman were driving off the base Spellman winced in pain. “How dare they cut my finger off. I’ll see them all dead.” “Try and relax we’ll sew it back on you’ll be just fine. Are you really planning on sharing the pot with those maniacs?” “Well son I don’t see how we have a choice. You did hear the part about them killing every living thing in town? We have no escape the town is sealed by troops. There is no other way.” “When we get to the hospital I’ll fix you up then we’ll go back to your house, torch the squirrels and head back to the hospital. I'm sure the fire department will want to speak with me." "But what about my house?" "We'll leave the gas on that way when Jenkins' men come to torch it we'll get a couple of them back for what they did to you." Sam had gone to the restroom and didn't hear that part.

Alex decided not to chance going out. Jenkins would have his men all over looking for him. He hoped Cecil didn't run into any trouble. Five minutes later Cecil returned. "How is it out there Cecil," Alex asked? "They have pictures of you everywhere. The troops are telling people that they're here to keep things in line at the fair tomorrow." "Hand me those bags, Renee I need your help in the kitchen. Everyone else get some sleep we have an early start in the morning. Good night," Alex told them all. "Mr. Peterson you go lay down with your family." Hank was tired so he did just that. Alex still hadn't said what the freezer bags were for but Hank knew he'd find out first thing in the morning. Renee, Cecil, Craig and Alex stayed up most of the night loading weapons and making out alternate plans in case something went wrong. Renee would go with the Peterson's. Alex and Cecil would go after Jenkins and Craig would clear a way out of town.

Going stitched Spellman's pinky back on. He told the head nurse he was going to take him home and that he'd be back. Then it hit him he could fake their deaths. When Jenkins men came to torch Spellman's house they would be blown up. No one would ever be able to tell it wasn't him and Going. He thought what did it matter the whole town would be dead tomorrow? Spellman was a little high from the painkillers Going had given him. It was getting late, now was the time to destroy the squirrels in the hospital. He still didn't want to leave any trace of the research. The bombs probably wouldn't destroy all of the buildings so he had to be sure. No use in having a worldwide manhunt for him or scaring off potential buyers.

Going and Spellman carried two five-gallon cans of gasoline thru the tunnel. Once they got to the end they put on the suits. They were both nervous the squirrels were gnawing loudly giving both men the shakes. "Are you sure this spray is going to work again," Spellman asked? "It better," Going said. They sprayed each other completely down with the toxin. The lights were blinking but they seemed different this night. Outside the lights appeared to be bouncing off of the giant tree carving of the squirrel. It was as if this was the mother squirrel and she knew someone was trying to harm her babies. It was drizzling earlier but now suddenly there was a heavy downpour. The rumbling rolled across the sky of Newton and was followed by lightning that lit the sky. Going and Spellman stood still then Going said, "come on we don't have much time." He reached down and opened the door. "BOOM, CRACK" the thunder and lightning seemed to rock the whole house. "Hurry," Spellman said. They walked in the lab.

The squirrels were in a frenzy gnawing and jumping all around. There was one who didn't move. They could see his beady eyes staring them down. They hurried and emptied the two cans of gasoline. "Okay, that's it let's get out of here." Just as Spellman opened the door one of the squirrels landed on his back. He screamed Going snatched it off and threw it against the wall. They got out and closed the door. "Are you alright, did it bite you," Going asked? "I don't think so," Spellman answered. "Let's get out of these suits and torch this place." After taking the suit off, Going took a piece of paper from his pocket lit it with a lighter, cracked the door and dropped it. The room went up in a blaze in a matter of seconds. The squirrels made awful sounds that seemed like they could be heard miles away. The two men ran down the tunnel and locked the entrance. Spellman grabbed some notes and pictures from a drawer. Going cut the gas line from the furnace and the two men rushed out of the house into the storm. They got in the car and drove off. Two of Jenkins men were watching from across the street. They called Jenkins and Sam answered, "it's done." "Good you know what to do." Sam walked down the hall and knocked on the door. "Come in," Jenkins said. Sam entered and told him, "it's done." "And our good doctor's Sam, what have they been chatting about?" "The bug fell off while Going was fixing up Spellman's finger." "Okay set up a perimeter two miles wide around the hospital no media. No one but the fire department," Jenkins ordered. "Let's get over to the hospital." "Yes sir," Sam replied. Sam gave Jenkins' orders to his men and the two of them headed for the hospital. Spellman and Going were already on their way. Jenkins' other men were pouring gasoline all over Spellman's house.

The rain had slowed down, the thunder and lightning had stopped. "Okay," one of the men said, "that should do it." The other said, "Do you smell something?" "No, give me a light," the man answered. "Sure," he took out a cigarette and put it in his mouth. He pulled out some matches and struck a match. Boom! The explosion brought the whole house down and rocked the other nearby homes. A big ball of fire that could be seen for miles shot up in the air. The troops on the highway in back of the house though they were miles away, felt the ground tremble. "What was that," they asked each other? Jenkins and Sam had been listening on the walkie-talkie. Jenkins knew what had happen. "Fucking bastards they set us up Sam. No matter they still need us to get out of town!" Jenkins got on his radio and ordered all his men to keep there present positions.

Chapter 45

It was 4:30, Alex and the rest of the people at the Peterson home heard the loud boom. Hank had been lying awake woken by the storm. It reminded him of the storm he and Terrez ran into that day over on Somerset. That's when he noticed the squirrel in front of Spellman's house. Alex shouted to everyone in the house. "Time to get up people. Time to get moving. Ronda fixed a quick bite for everyone." Alex told Cecil to get an open line and see what was going on. They heard about the fire at the hospital and the explosion in a residential area not far from the highway. "Craig this is it our chance, get moving." Craig got his gear took one of the trucks and left. The rest of them got a bite to eat and listened in on all the commotion at the hospital over the walkie-talkies. Cecil had tapped in on an open frequency. “Let’s move Cecil,” Alex said. “Renee you know what to do. Good luck people.” Alex and Cecil took off in the early morning mist that set in over Newton. “What now Hank asked?” “We wait and at six we move out.” “Are you sure about this,” Ronda asked? “Honey, we don’t have a choice,” Renee said. “Everyone get suited you all know the plan,” she told them. Ronda looked at Hank. He went up to her and gave her a hug. “Everything is going to be fine.” By the time they suited and loaded up the van it was six on the nose. Renee had given everyone a refresher course on how everything worked.

Craig parked about a mile from where the troops were set up. There were only a few trucks tending to the fire at Spellman’s house. He had set some explosives in the area to give the appearance of other gas lines rupturing. He was set and in place with his infrared glasses. The perimeter where he was at had about thirty men. Most of the men were laid back watching the smoke in the air. He looked at his watch and started the count down, five, four, three, two, one. He located the radioman and had his aim right between his eyes. Boom, another explosion it covered up the noise from the shot. The private fell back and most of the others moved forward toward the explosion. He gunned them down with an automatic weapon. They fell like ducks in an arcade-shooting machine. There was another explosion. The last of his bombs went off in the residential area covering up the slaughter of the troops. At the same time, he fired a rocket launcher at the remaining men. He had done his part. He walked down the highway looking for any survivors. Spotting one, he picked the injured man up and carried him to what used to be the perimeter. He moved the dead bodies aside and took hold of the radio. On a separate line he called in. "All clear Alex, route 99 is open." "Copy, that's good work," Alex said. "Do you?" "Yes, I still have one alive in case Jenkins calls."

Vendors in all the hotels were up now loading their vans and trucks for the big fair. Cecil spotted one of the early birds coming down the road. "I've got one Alex two miles and approaching." They pulled their van into the middle of the street, put the hazard lights on and stopped the van. Once the van stopped Alex walked up and said, "How you folks doing? Are you folk's vendors too?" "Yes, we have one of the hot dog stands," the driver said. "What about you?" "Got the ice cream but our batteries are dead sure could use a jump." "No problem," the driver said. Cecil opened the passenger door and had his gun pointed at the ladies head. Alex pulled the driver out of the van. "Listen close folks we're not here to harm you. We're going to take your place. Take our truck head for route 99 and get the hell out of town. Do not attempt to call for help, do not stop for anything. Step over here both of you." Alex watched them at gunpoint while Cecil loaded all of the artillery into the vendor's van. "It's a matter of your life and death, now get moving," Alex told them. The two frightened vendors did just what he said.

Hank, Renee, and Ronda were coming down the road. Alex called in, "where are you?" "About a mile from you, we see the lights." Hank pulled over and Alex gave them the vendor papers. "You should be all set now." "We're fine but you better get going daylight is approaching fast." Alex and Cecil headed for the base. The Peterson's and Renee went to the fair grounds, found their vendor spot and began to set up the hot dog stand. This was the perfect way not to be noticed and be close without drawing attention to them.

The fire department was at the hospital. Jenkins got with the fire chief and offered his assistance. Smoke was plummeting though the hospital and everyone was moved down to the lower floors. Going and Spellman were there and showed the chief to the stairway that had been closed off. This made it easy for his men to get to the sixth floor where the smoke and fire burned at a massive rate. The sprinklers on that floor had been shut off years ago so everything up there was totally destroyed. After about an hour, they had the fire out and there was no threat of danger to the rest of the patients on the floors below. The fire chief told Going they suspected arson and had found what appeared to be bones but weren't sure. He told them he would give him a full report within twenty-four hours. Jenkins was standing right there and heard the whole conversation. The chief thanked him for his help and mentioned the fire on route 99. "Yes," Jenkins said, "something about a house exploding. I'll radio my men and tell them to give you any assistance you need." "No need Captain we just got a report that it's all under control. Thanks again for your help."

Sam had Spellman in the truck. Jenkins told Going to come with him. “Do you think I’m a fucking idiot? One more stunt like that and I’ll blow your brains out. Get in the truck let’s go.” They got in the truck, “Sam patch me in to the unit over on 99.” Sam called, “this is unit one come in.” Craig put a gun to the injured private’s head, instructed him to tell them everything was alright and that the fire had been put out. “What’s your status there?” Craig pressed the gun deeper into the private’s right temple. “Everything here checks out sir the fire is out and we’re still in position. The fire department is headed the other way sir.” “Hold your position private and remember no one in and no one out. Do you copy?” This time Craig pressed the barrel of the gun under his throat. “Yes sir I copy, out.” Alex came on, “Craig do you see the van?” “Yes Alex I have them in sight. The fire department drove right by them they’re coming to me now.” The fire was miles ahead so nobody saw the dead bodies scattered all over the highway. The couple pulled up. Craig pointed the gun at them and told them to go ahead and don’t look back. “Remember, it’s a matter of life or death, your life or death,” he said.

Jenkins was back at the base. He had a grin on his face like the culprit that had successfully stolen candy from a baby. But now was the time for real action. He still hadn't found Alex or Renee Ward. He called a meeting in one of the makeshift rooms of the base. Sam, Going, Spellman, the Mayor and some of his trained top men were there. Sam and three men were to accompany the mayor to the fair. After the speech, they would head for the safe spot where the chopper would pick them up. All the others would drive out before the bombs were !aunched. "Is everyone clear on this," Jenkins asked as he lit another cigar? "Clear," the whole room responded. "Then let's move out!" Sam took the mayor with him. Jenkins demanded that Going and Spellman stay with him. He locked them in a room, left a couple of men outside and headed for the chopper, which had just arrived.

It was seven thirty and the sun was out promising a beautiful day. All the vendors for the fair were in place open and ready to go. A lot of the townspeople were at their homes preparing for one of the biggest days of the year for Newton, Iowa. Hank and Renee were in the vendor booth. They were prepared to serve the public, slip them little fliers about the danger they were in and how to get out of town. Ronda and the kids would work the crowd. They planned on just simply taking the mike from the mayor to warn those who had not yet been warned.

Alex and Cecil watched the chopper land and were checking it out. They had lost the frequency and didn't know Jenkins' whole plan. They knew he still had Going and Spellman inside the base. One of them had to get in there, Alex thought to himself. Cecil tapped him on his shoulder. "Got him!" They could see Jenkins heading for the chopper. "I need it now Cecil." "Alex you better take a look at this." Cecil pointed out to Alex the pilot examining the missile launchers. "Alex, do you see what I see?" "Yes Cecil I do." In the binoculars you could clearly see the code 2TLNB on the missile. "Motherfucker," Alex said out loud. "I've got to get to that chopper." Jenkins headed back for the base. The pilot turned the chopper off and followed. "This is it Cecil cover me."

Alex managed his way to the outside of the base in the direction the pilot was now headed. He hid on the side of the chopper. As the pilot approached him, he grabbed him, broke his neck and got into his clothes. He prayed this would work and that Jenkins wouldn't recognize him. Once inside he found his way to the room where Jenkins was on the phone with General Cross. He had his walkie-talkie on so Cecil could hear. Jenkins turned to him and said, "Where have you been?" "Sorry Captain, I had to take a dunk. Got any coffee around here?" "Take him to the room with the others and make sure he doesn't wander off." Jenkins ordered one of his men. "The rest of you start breaking down this base we move out in fifteen." "I need to make some last minute checks on our cargo, sir." "Fine," he pointed at one of his men, "go with him and then take him to the waiting room with the others." The voice came over the phone. "Captain Jenkins are you there?" "Yes sir, General, we're all set to go at noon instead of one, sir. I just need your clearance, sir." That was the last thing Alex heard as he walked out the door and headed back to the chopper. He hoped Cecil had got all of the information.

Alex didn't dare over power Jenkins' man. He went to the chopper, looked over the controls, checked out the missile launchers and hoped he'd be able to fly the thing. Cecil called in the information he had overheard to the others. They only had two hours left. The mayor was due to give his speech at eleven. It was ten o'clock now.

Chapter 46

Most of the people at the fair were just throwing away the warning notes and enjoying the fair. They thought it was some type of prank being played by kids. “We have to get ready to make our move, if they go earlier than what Cecil just told us we’re all fucked. I’m going to go take a look around. I’ll be right back.” “Hurry half these people are infected and don’t even know it or they will be soon. Hank, take a look over there.” There was a man near a dumpster puking his guts out.

Ronda and the kids had strayed away from the zone they were given and that’s who Hank was going after. He got about a hundred feet away from them when he saw the squirrels starting to gather. Some were in the trees and others on the ground. He slowly headed back to the booth.

Terrez saw them too and told his mother. They headed for the parking lot toward the van. Suddenly a voice came over the loud speaker. It was the mayor. They were going even earlier than expected.

"Good morning," the voice said. "Welcome to the tenth annual Newton, Iowa county fair." Sam was behind him looking over the crowd. That's when he spotted Renee. "Got her sir, he whispered into his wireless headphone mike." "Good bring her to me." Sam motioned, two men walked up to Renee and took her to the awaiting car. Sam joined them leaving a man with the mayor. Hank saw all of this and headed for the platform toward the mike. He motioned the man watching the mayor down and shot him in the leg. Hank jumped up on stage grabbed the mike and told the people of Newton to get out of town.

At that same moment, the squirrels started attacking. The crowd started screaming and running. Ronda and the kids barely made it to the van. "Where's Hank," she screamed? Hank had run and closed himself in one of the vendor booths. He was safe for now. "I think he's in that booth over there," Porter said. "It looked like I saw someone jump in and close the front of it." The squirrels were killing everything out in the open that moved. A little baby was being ripped apart in his carriage. The mother had tried to shield him from the squirrels with her body but there were to many of them. They ripped her body apart.

Ronda pulled the van to the booth that Porter had seen someone duck into and blew the horn. Other people had made it to their cars, some with squirrels attached to them and biting them. They were hitting other cars and running over people who were in the way. The place looked like a feeding ground with thousands of live snacks. Hank heard the horn blowing and peeked outside. "Yes!" He set fire to the booth and made it to the van that was only a few feet away. The kids opened the side door and he dove in. One of the squirrels had bitten him on the leg. He wrapped it up and told Ronda to let him drive.

He could see the car Sam snatched Renee into leaving the parking lot. Blood fell from above where people were being eaten while trapped on the rides. Some chose to jump to their deaths rather than sit a hundred feet in the air on the Ferris wheel while being feasted upon. Hank made it out of the parking lot and was following the car. "Everyone set here," he asked? "Yes," everyone said. "Okay then do it now."

The kids and Ronda pulled out their guns and started shooting at the car in front of them. "What the fuck," Sam said. He had taken his eyes off Renee. The other two men started shooting back at the van. Ronda and the girls were screaming and ducking. "Stop shooting!" "No keep on shooting," Terrez hollered. That's when Hank took a bullet in the arm. He almost lost control of the van. Renee managed to get her gun out and shot the driver in the back of the head. The car crashed, Sam put a gun to her head and snatched her out the car. Hank stopped the van. "Get out now all of you or I'll blow her brains out right here!"

The mayor had been shot during the ordeal and wasn't going to make it so Sam told one of his men to bring the mayor to him. He made the mayor and Renee kneel in front of him. "Throw out your weapons now he ordered." No one moved. "On the count of three I'll kill her, One, two, three." Boom! the shot rang out. The mayor fell flat on his face. Hank threw his weapon out, as did everyone else in the van. "Okay kids this is it be brave." The other two men went and got them out the van. "Line them up over there," Sam shouted. "Give me that radio. Jenkins come in. We've got them, sir." "Good," Jenkins said, "kill them all and get outside the perimeter. We launch in fifteen minutes."

Sam picked Renee up and placed her with the others. Ronda was crying so were a few of the kids. Hank looked at Renee and she just nodded her head. "Well now," Sam said, "I'd love to stay and chat but we have a chopper to catch." He took his automatic rifle and aimed straight at Hank's heart. All you heard were the firing of his rifle and Sam screaming like a madman. "Shoot at me you little fucking bastards. I'll blow your fucking little hearts out." Blood flew everywhere as he did just that. He shot every one of them in the chest area. "Blow their hearts out!" They all fell in a pool of blood. Sam was standing over them now. "I should blow the bitch's head off." He pointed the gun at Renee's head. Then one of the other men grabbed him, "come on," said, "their all dead. We only have ten minutes left." "Right, we have to take their van lets go," Sam said.

Chapter 47

Sam and his men headed for the location where they were to be picked up. He called Jenkins. “It’s done but the mayor didn’t make it.” Alex, Jenkins, Going’s, and Spellman were airborne now. Alex was flying the chopper. He could feel Jenkins staring at him. They could see the squirrels feasting on the bodies and those who had made it to their cars heading down the different streets in town. He ordered his men to shoot anyone trying to pass the perimeters surrounding the town. “This is it gentleman. Pilot I want four of those missiles fired right in the locations I gave you earlier.” “No sir, I won’t do it I have friends down there.” “What, that’s a direct order fire those missiles now,” Jenkins said. Alex refused and Jenkins put a gun to his head you have until the count of three Mister. Alex pulled off his helmet. “It’s you Alex Reed I should have known.” “Captain who is this man,” Going asked? “Shut up,” Jenkins told him. Cecil was following the chopper. Alex had a tracker on him. “Okay Alex, you win,” then Going shouted, “look out!” Alex pulled up he almost hit an Icy-Hot pain reliever billboard. Jenkins shot him in the side causing Alex to fall forward. “Grab him and pull him off the controls you two!” The chopper was spinning out of control. Spellman and Going snatched his body off the controls. Jenkins took the seat belt off Alex and threw him out of the chopper. Jenkins got control of the chopper just before they were about to run into some wires. He pulled up on the controls and circled around the target area. He would fire the missiles himself.

Alex had landed in a lake and Cecil was headed for him. Cecil jumped into the lake and fished him out. He was still alive but bleeding pretty bad. “I couldn’t stop him,” Alex said. “Don’t worry Craig is on his way.” Cecil put Alex in the truck, turned around and headed for route 99. At that moment, two loud explosions were heard followed by two more. Cecil was doing about a hundred and twenty miles an hour. Ten seconds after the explosions a cold arctic wind swept through Newton. It froze people running right in their tracks. The frozen bodies shattered into a frozen dust. The same thing happened to the squirrels. Glass blew out of the windows of homes and businesses. In a matter of ten minutes the arctic wind swept in freezing everything that moved in the town of Newton.

Chapter 48

Jenkins turned the chopper around and made it out of harms way. He set his men up close enough so that they would be killed also. He wasn't about to leave any witnesses. Sam and the other two men made it just in time and were safe. Jenkins landed the chopper and picked them up. They were just about to fly out of Iowa when Jenkins spotted a truck moving down route 99. "What the fuck is that? Who the fuck is that?" He circled around. There were two vans speeding down the highway. "Get them!" His men opened fire on the vans. They pulled over and took cover. Jenkins circled around again. Craig got out of the van. Cecil pulled Alex out of the other one and they took cover. "Don't blow it up just bring it down," Alex moaned. "Got it," Craig said. Just as Jenkins was about to fire upon them Craig fired a rocket launcher that took out the chopper's back rotor. The chopper whirled smoked and spun out of control. "Brace yourselves we're going down," Jenkins hollered. They landed with a loud crash and the flames started to build up. "You have to get the briefcase out before it explodes," Alex moaned. "Going has it." Jenkins, Sam, Going, Spellman and their two men crawled out of the burning chopper and opened fire on Alex and his team. Cecil and Craig returned the gunfire. "Draw their fire away from the vans. Cover me." Craig took one in the leg while running across the road. Cecil shot one of Jenkins men in the head then ran across the road to help Craig. Alex had crawled away from the van. Sam pointed out a shed about twenty yards away. "Take them over there I'll finish this," Jenkins ordered. Sam told the two doctors to run and not to stop until they were behind the shed. They took off and Alex opened fire. He shot the other man in the back and the man fell dead. "Alex, I'm coming for you," Jenkins shouted.

Sam, Going and Spellman made it to the back of the shed and took cover. Going still had the briefcase with the files in his hand. Spellman was hysterical, "we have to get out of here," he screamed. The chopper blew up. When the smoke cleared Jenkins was standing over Alex with a gun pointed to his head. "This time I won't miss old friend," he said, as he cocked the gun. A gunshot went off and Alex lay still. Jenkins fell over with a bullet though the back of his neck. He was bleeding like someone had sliced his throat and then he fell dead.

Through the smoke Hank had crept up on Sam and the doctors. Sam was just about to react when Ronda put a gun to his head. "I wish you would you motherfucker, drop it." Renee had a gun pointed at Going and Spellman, "well now if it isn't the two witch doctors from hell." "Cecil, Craig, go and get Alex he's in pretty bad shape. Well now Sam I should blow your fucking heart out," Hank said. "But, I have a better idea you murderous son of bitches." Bam! The gunshot rung through the air, "I prefer the brain." Hank turned and walked away with Ronda following. "The information I have here is worth billions." Going said to Renee. "You don't have to do this." "He's right we can all live like kings and queens, there's enough for everyone," Spellman said. "Oh really and does that count the thousands of people you just murdered in Newton," Renee asked? BAM! BAM!

Chapter 49

Renee called Bear Russell and told him what had happen. “You know I can never come back Bear.” “I know but what about the files what happen?” “Goodbye Bear,” she said and hung up the phone.

It was a sunny day and things were great in the Cayman’s. The kids were at the beach swimming and Hank was basking in the sun drinking his favorite, Margarita. Ronda was reading one of her science fiction thrillers.

Chapter 50

(Flashback)

"Well now, I'd love to stay and chat but we have a chopper to catch," Sam said. He took his automatic rifle and aimed straight at Hank's heart. Sam and his men left the bodies there. They didn't pay much attention to the truck that passed them because they knew there was no escape from Newton. Craig had watched the whole thing. He followed once he left the fairgrounds. After Sam tried to execute them he prayed they were Okay. It had been a long shot but the only way out. When Hank had gone to the sheriff's shed Alex asked him if they saw any bulletproof vest. They had found some vest. Hank wondered what the blood from the blood bank was for. The final thing was the freezer bags. They taped blood filled freezer bags onto the outside of every ones vest. They were sore and some of them took a few nicks and wounds but that scheme saved their lives. He would always be grateful for that. The sheriff's wife and the rest of his family had been sent airline tickets to the Cayman Islands. They all accepted, even though they were not sure where the tickets had come from. After Alex got back to the Hughes Estate there was still one small thing missing. Volen Hughes had bought fifty one percent of the shares of (CBR). Renee had switched briefcases and when the rest of the family arrived in the Caymans, Volen transferred a nice amount of money and he received his files. There was only one question that troubled Hank and Renee. HAD ALL THE SQUIRRELS REALLY BEEN DESTROYED?

About the Author

Hank Patterson is a native Detroiter who attended Mumford High School and Wayne State University. Hank and his family love to travel to the islands and still reside in the Metro Detroit area. Hank, from early childhood wrote numerous short stories and scripts. A masterful storyteller, Hank has put it all together in his first book of soon to be many. His passion for horror is sure to please horror fans everywhere. So sit back in your favorite sofa or chair and get ready for, ***"Squirrels the Mutation."***

Printed in the United States
17141LVS00003B/1-66

9 781414 032092